CYNTHIA HICKEY

MOUNTAIN REDEMPTION

CYNTHIA HICKEY

ISBN-13: 978-1-0881-4802-0

DEDICATION

Thank you to God, my family and my fans. None of this would be possible without you. Also, thank you to my dad for telling me about my relatives taking axes to the moonshiners trucks.

It made for a great scene.

1

A gunshot shattered the brisk autumn day, piercing the late-afternoon silence.

Phoebe Lillie's head jerked up, and she raised a hand to shade her eyes, peering over the hills of Pine Ridge. She frowned. Surely that wasn't Pa still hunting.

Grandma Edna paused in climbing the knoll and stooped to pluck something from the travel-worn path leading to the cabin. A cry of alarm escaped her.

She bustled forward and handed Phoebe a straight pin. "Evil's a-coming. This had the point aimed right at me."

"Then you should have left it lie." Phoebe rolled her eyes at her grandmother's superstition.

"No, no, can't do that. That would bring worse luck. Where's your sense, girl? Nineteen-years-old and you don't know something simple like that?"

She brushed past Phoebe into the dim recesses of the cabin. "Where's the young'uns?"

"Chores." Phoebe left the door open to allow the breeze to circulate and clutched her worn sweater closer. Her baby sister wailed from the front room. "Maggie's waking now, Grandma."

The sound of another gunshot ricocheted across the Hollow. Grandma put a hand to her bosom. "That noise is going to send me to an early grave. Where's your pa? It can't be him hunting. He most likely finished hours ago. It's almost suppertime."

"I'm getting worried. Pa told me he wanted to get started cutting the Timothy grass tomorrow. There's no way he should still be hunting." Phoebe bent and lifted one-year-old Maggie from a pallet on the floor. She wrinkled her nose against the strong odor wafting from the wet diaper.

"Talk around Dixon's store is that the selling of moonshine is on the rise." Grandma lowered herself into her rocking chair. "Anyways, he's going to have someone deliver the sugar and batteries. Gave us a fair price for the eggs and butter too."

Phoebe glanced upward. *Thank you, Lord, but please curb Grandma's spending. Christmas isn't far away, and the little ones will be expecting a gift.*

If something happened to Pa, the holidays would be leaner than usual. Another hardship thrust on Phoebe. They wouldn't survive the holiday season with another parent gone. Losing Ma had been hard enough, leaving a hole in the family that Phoebe could never fill.

Maggie gurgled at her, reaching to twine her pudgy fingers in Phoebe's hair. The baby's smile wrenched Phoebe's heart. She looked so much like their ma. Pa hadn't held the baby once since Ma died birthing her. Never cuddled her soft skin or been on the receiving end of a gummy smile. Nothing. He missed so much.

Unease slithered along her back. Gooseflesh prickled her arms. Phoebe shivered, hugging the baby to her chest. She'd experienced the same feeling the night Maggie was born. Something had happened to Pa. She knew it as clear as if a newspaper printed the story on the front page.

Phoebe jolted as her other siblings burst through the door, clamoring for supper. After handing Maggie to her sixteen-year-old sister, Viola, Phoebe limped to the window. Pa had left before sunup. Now, the sun began its crimson descent over the mountain. For the first time, the familiar sound of gunshots sent tremors through her. She sighed and closed the door.

Viola tied Maggie into a straight-back chair with a dishtowel around the baby's waist then started setting the table. Phoebe cut cornbread and poured glasses full of buttermilk. She cast anxious glances toward Pa's chair at the head of the table. Ma's chair remained as empty as the day she died.

No one sat there or claimed the spot of woman of the house. It was time. Once she'd finished serving the seven others, she straightened her back and took Ma's seat next to Pa's.

The others stared for a moment then transferred their attentions to their plates. Grandma nodded and smiled. Phoebe relaxed. The time had come to take her mother's place.

She glanced around the table. If her premonitions about Pa were correct, it'd be up to her and her seventy-two-year-old grandmother to make sure the children reached adulthood, a difficult task in the Ozark Mountains, even with two parents. Phoebe's shoulders slumped.

The chunks of cornbread swam in the cold milk. Her stomach rebelled at the sight of the too common meal. Her family spooned the simple dinner into hungry mouths. She should've cooked beans to go with it or made one of her sisters cook.

She eyed her quilting frame hanging from the ceiling. On the floor under it sat a box of quilt squares waiting to be sewn. She couldn't do everything. Not and finish the work that actually brought in money.

Footsteps sounded on the wood-planked front porch. Phoebe's heart leaped. It could be Pa.

James rose and slid the beam holding the door closed. He turned with a grin. "It's Eli Coffman with the sugar."

Why Eli? Anyone but him.

Grandma's toothless smile stretched her wrinkled face. "Chocolate gravy for breakfast."

Cheers rose around the table. Phoebe sighed.

Eli entered with a ten pound bag of sugar in one hand and batteries in the other. His muddy-brown eyes fixed on Phoebe. Revulsion gnawed a hole in her stomach. "I got over here as quick as I could. Had to feed the little ones first."

Phoebe forced a greeting on her lips. "We've corn bread and fresh buttermilk." *Please don't stay.* She couldn't bear to look at him over her kitchen table.

He shook his head. "I thank you kindly, but I'd best be getting back."

Relief flooded through her.

"Walk him out, Phoebe." Grandma waved her fork.

Curse proper manners. Stifling a groan, Phoebe stood and sidestepped around Eli. The stench of sour corn mash rolled off him. She swallowed against the bile rising in her throat and stormed outside. The chilly night air slapped her flushed cheeks. She drew in deep, cleansing breaths.

Eli brushed past her, his hand trailing down her arm as he went to stand on the bottom step and peered up at her. "Have you done some more thinking on my proposal? My little ones need a ma."

"So do my brothers and sisters." She crossed her arms.

Eli's eyes hardened. "Still holding out for love? Like there's a flock of men willing to marry a woman with a gimpy leg, no matter how comely her features?"

She raised her chin and wished for the shotgun propped in the corner of the dining room. "You can leave now. Your little ones are home alone." Phoebe moved inside, shutting the door behind her. She leaned against the rough wood and closed her eyes.

A left leg only an inch shorter than the other didn't cause any more problems than back-ache at the end of a busy day. If a man couldn't love her despite her handicap, he could go to the devil. "JJ, light the lamp and put the batteries in the radio. The Hay's weekly broadcast comes on in a few minutes."

James's face lit up. "You sure we can spare them?"

She nodded. "There's little enough pleasure in the world." Phoebe shuffled to the sink where Viola had already filled it with steaming water from a kettle. Her hands stung as the heat melted away the outdoor chill, sending biting ants through her fingers.

"You're a fool for turning him down." Grandma's knitting needles clacked behind her.

"You're going to be an old maid. Can't afford to be choosy at your age."

Phoebe shrugged. If her pa didn't show up soon, she'd have more responsibility than she could handle without a husband tying her down. And a drunkard of a husband at that.

She lifted a glass from the soapy water and set it in a basin of clear water. Besides, her quilt-making and taking care of her siblings kept her busy enough. There was no time in Phoebe's life for a husband of her own.

*

Frigid mountain air tore at his clothing and bit at his cheeks as the sun disappeared over the craggy peaks of the Ozarks. Jacob Wright set his satchel down, hitched his pack higher on his shoulder, and then flexed his stiff fingers.

He shuffled along the road, rocks digging into the soles of his shoes. Weeks of riding the rails looking for work and preaching in whatever town would have him, had left him ragged and exhausted. He looked forward to the peace of Pine Ridge, Arkansas, and its simple people.

The tiny ad in Compton's newspaper asking for a teacher was a gift from heaven. At least he'd have a roof over his head, food to eat, and cash in his pocket. Not as much as when he'd been a deputy in Little Rock, but enough.

He shivered. Why didn't this little-known place

have a decent road in and out? He winced at his bitter thoughts. *Sorry, Lord, don't mean to complain.*

Jacob glanced at his watch. Nine o'clock. No wonder lights flickered off in windows of the shack and cabin windows he passed. He needed to find Dixon's store, an impossible task on a moonless night. Staying out in the cold didn't appeal to him. He'd stop at the next home he came to and beg the occupants to lend him a corner to sleep in.

A light flickered through the trees. A dog barked. Jacob jerked. Sounded close. He searched the trees.

There … a small cabin nestled among the oaks and pines. Smoke curled from the chimney like vapors. Well, at least someone was home. A red-bone hound bounded toward him.

He held out his palm to the dog. "Good boy. I'm just looking for a place to lay my head. Hey, the house!"

"Who's there?" A woman's voice came to him through an open window.

"I'm the new school teacher, ma'am. I'm afraid I'm lost."

The door opened, silhouetting what appeared to be a child holding a rifle as big as her. He'd definitely stepped into another world when friendly folks were greeted with a gun. "Stay where you are. I haven't heard about a teacher."

"I'm supposed to report to a Jim Dixon."

"You've got the wrong place. He's about a half-mile down Possum Road."

Was everything named after an animal? "Please. I've come a long way. I'm looking for a warm place to lie down."

"Let him in, child. Dixon told me a teacher would be arriving." An older woman's voice rang out as glorious as angels singing to Jacob's tired body.

The girl lowered her rifle and ushered him inside. Jacob stepped into the warm glow from the fire and gaped. She wasn't just a girl, but the prettiest yellow-haired woman he'd ever seen. He closed his mouth before she thought him an idiot. He thrust out his hand. "I'm Jacob Wright."

Eyes shining like polished buttons peered at him then glared at his hand for a moment before slipping her fingers in his and giving a quick shake. "Phoebe Lillie. This is my grandma, Edna Lillie. Everyone calls her Grandma. We've some cornbread left from supper if you're hungry."

His stomach grumbled in response. A hint of a smile teased the corners of her mouth. "I'll get some cold milk from the cellar to go with it."

"I'm much obliged." Jacob dropped his belongings near the door and took a seat on one of the benches running beside the simple kitchen table.

A potbellied stove provided warmth and served

to cook the meals. A pump over a metal bucket occupied the center of a wide wood counter. Shelves lined the wall on both sides of a small window. Yellow-checked calico served as curtains. Rag rugs littered the floor, providing cheerful color on the worn planks. A quilting rack with a partial quilt hung suspended from the ceiling. A rocking chair and a few straight backed ones with straw-woven seats, provided places to rest. A ladder led to an overhead loft, and two doors flanked the fireplace. A home holding necessities only, with simple touches of a woman's attempt toward a comfortable feel.

"Is the man of the house home?" he asked.

Phoebe's back straightened. "He's hunting." Pensive lines on the sides of her mouth deepened as she glanced toward the door. "Ought to be back at any time."

"Stop being prickly, girl," Grandma Edna said. "My nose was itching all day. I knew someone would be coming to our door needing sustenance."

"Grandma, please. Enough of the superstitions." Phoebe handed Jacob a plate.

"It's fact, missy." Grandma crossed her arms.

Jacob bit back a grin. He remembered the warnings about these country people and their superstitions. Which one did Grandma refer too? An itchy nose signified a visitor with a hole in his britches. Well, that fit him to a tee.

"Thank you." He crumbled his cornbread into his glass and scooped a spoonful into his mouth. Soggy, but bounty from heaven to his starving body.

Phoebe nodded and wrapped a shawl tighter around her. It wasn't until then he noticed the patched cotton nightgown she wore. The fire's rays outlined her curvy shape beneath the fabric. Heat rushed to Jacob's face, and his hand paused before he ducked his head. "I'm sorry. I disturbed your rest."

"Nonsense. It's the Christian thing for us to do." The creak of the wood rocking chair brought his gaze up. Grandma set a folded, faded quilt on the table beside him. "Make yourself at home. In the morning, we'll point you in the right direction."

"Much obliged. God bless." He kept his attention focused on the food in front of him until the ladies retired to the loft overhead.

Having finished eating, he stood and set his dishes in the tub of water, then dug his Bible out of his pack. Hunkered down in front of the dying fire, he tried to read his daily quota of Proverbs.

Who were these people giving him shelter? Wary, yet welcoming. Poor, yet willing to give up what little they had to a stranger. He closed the book and stared into the scarlet embers. He turned off the oil lamp. He wouldn't waste their precious resources.

There had to be a way to repay their kindness without ruffling any feathers. Maybe cutting wood. He studied his hands. Work-worn and calloused, yet they hadn't held an axe in a long time. Nothing much more than a pencil stub. Or a gun. That wasn't the life for him anymore. He refocused his attention on his new job as a teacher. An occupation more fitting for a follower of Christ.

People this simple wouldn't have much in the way of teaching tools. What would he use to train up the children of Pine Ridge? He didn't even know if the place had a schoolhouse. He hoped it did. A smarter man might have thought to ask before accepting the job.

He pulled the quilt off the table and wrapped it around his shoulders before settling into one of the chairs. It might be an uncomfortable night, but at least he'd be warm. Jacob fell asleep dreaming of a golden-haired beauty with curves to set a man's mind racing, and fear haunting her face.

2

"Viola." Phoebe shook her sister and peeled back the Rose of Sharon quilt from the bed. "Milk the cow and be quiet about it. We've a guest sleeping downstairs."

"Ooh." Viola's squeal nearly pierced Phoebe's eardrum as her sister leaped from the mattress and peered over the railing. "A man. A handsome one, too. Why's he still sleeping?" Her wide-eyed gaze slid to Phoebe. "Only city slickers sleep this late, I reckon."

"As if you weren't doing the same thing. Put your eyes back in your head and get busy on your chores. Once the children wake, they'll want that chocolate gravy Grandma promised them. And there'll be no end to their pestering." Phoebe pulled her nightgown off over her head and hung it on a hook nailed into the wall. She grabbed her blue-flowered housedress, threw it on, shoved her feet into her scuffed brown shoes, and donned her ratty brown sweater, before climbing down the ladder.

Viola stared at the sleeping Jacob Wright. "He's like an angel with the fire casting a halo around his head. He's wearing pin striped pants and a tie! A city feller thrust into the midst of us common folk. Who is he? What color are his eyes?"

"Stop it." Phoebe gritted her teeth. "He's the new school teacher, and I don't know what color his eyes are. Now, git." She shoved her sister toward the door. "The sooner you get the milking done, the sooner you can ogle him." If Phoebe didn't keep her busy with chores, that is. A shoulder-load of work was all that would keep Viola from making a fool of herself. That girl would be the death of her, drooling over every man in long pants.

What color are his eyes? She snorted. Like she'd noticed after he'd come in long past dark last night.

Phoebe shook her head and went to the counter to mix the flour, sugar, and cocoa for the gravy. She'd hoped to save the precious ingredients for Thanksgiving Day, but once Grandma got her hands on sugar, there was no turning back. It was a wonder the woman had any teeth left.

Where was Pa? With him gone, how long would their funds last?

"Can I help with anything?" A deep baritone sounded behind her.

"Oh." Phoebe turned, scattering flour across the front of her. She glared at Jacob.

"I'm sorry I startled you." One corner of his mouth lifted, sending butterflies through her stomach.

His eyes were as green and alluring as a spring field. Heat flooded her face and she turned back to preparing breakfast. "My ma would roll over in her grave if I were to allow a guest to work. You sit. I'll be finished shortly. After you eat, JJ will show you to Dixon's store."

"Will JJ be one of my students?"

Phoebe nodded. "If he wants. He's fifteen. There's three of school age here in the family. But JJ thinks he's a man." She glanced at the deer antlers over the fireplace. The missing shotgun made her heart sink. If Pa didn't show up soon, JJ might well become the man of the house. If Pa didn't show by mid-day, she'd scour the woods.

Jacob leaned against the table. "I couldn't help but notice your limp. Are you hurt?"

Phoebe set her jaw and turned to face him. She twisted a dishtowel in her hands and fought the urge to put the nosy stranger in his place. "I broke it when I was young. The bone didn't heal properly."

"Have you thought about putting a lift in one shoe? Or building up the heel?"

She stiffened. Obviously, city folk didn't know when to mind their own business. "We've other things to occupy our time."

"I could do it for you. I've a little skill with

wood." He bent and lifted her left foot in his hands.

Phoebe jerked free, stumbling against the counter. "How dare you?"

"It's only a matter of making one shoe heel thicker." He reached for her again. "I'd like to return the favor for your hospitality."

Grandma shuffled into the room and cackled as she lowered into the rocking chair. "Mister, you ain't got the sense God gave a goose. Up here, we don't touch people without asking, we don't offer to pay for services God expects us to give, and most men back away when Phoebe's got her dander up."

He turned a bright shade of crimson and held up his hands. "I meant no harm."

"Apology accepted." Grandma lowered her round figure into a chair.

Didn't Phoebe have a say in whether she accepted his apology or not? She snorted and turned back to her work. Her leg tingled where he'd touched her. Even through her wool stockings. No one other than family had ever laid hands on her. Yet, it wasn't unpleasant. Did that make her as wanton as she feared Viola would turn out? Or did she have an attraction for the stranger? She couldn't. Her skin prickled. The sooner the man went about his own way, the better for the Lillie family. None of them had need of fancy city ideas. A block of wood in her shoe, ha!

"Give him your shoe, child."

Phoebe whirled and gaped at her grandma. "Excuse me?"

"Your shoe." Grandma flicked her hand as if she were waving off a fly. "While you've been lost in your daydreams, we've been discussing your predicament. I think this city school teacher might be on to something." She set the rocker in motion. "Come on. Take it off and stand in the center of the room so he can see you better."

Phoebe slipped off her shoes and stood as rigid as a Southern Pine while Jacob squatted next to her. She wanted to run for the protection of the trees. Why did Grandma insist on treating her like a child?

Using his hands, Jacob measured her from hip to toe. His hands skimmed her body, barely touching, yet every connection felt like a fiery brand. She sucked in her breath and closed her eyes, willing her heart to stay inside her ribcage where it belonged.

JJ ambled into the room. Rubbing sleep from his eyes, he yawned. He squinted at her and Mr. Wright. His eyes flared open. Hard lines etched along his face. His hand balled into a fist at his side. "What's that man doing to Phoebe?"

"Fixing her leg." Grandma slowed her rocking.

A light sprang into JJ's eyes. "No kidding?" He crowded closer, peering at Jacob as he worked.

One-by-one the other children trudged into the

room. They joined JJ staring at her like the freak of nature she was. She fought the tears. God could reach down now and take her home, and she wouldn't argue a word.

JJ thrust out his hand. "I'm James Lillie. People call me JJ. You ain't from around here, huh?"

Straightening, Jacob took her brother's hand. "No, but I'm hoping to be for a long time. I'm the new school teacher."

JJ pursed his lips and gave a sniff. "I can already read and do figures. Ain't got no need of further schooling. This farm is all I need to know."

"World's changing." Jacob carried Phoebe's shoes to the table. "Education becomes more important every year. A learned man can go far. If you do well, you can leap ahead of your neighbors."

JJ nodded. "I'll think on it."

Viola rushed inside, plunked down a bucket of milk on the counter, splashing some over the side, and leaned over Jacob's shoulder.

"Got a piece of wood about this size?" Jacob spread apart his fingers. "I'll attach it to the bottom of her shoe, paint it to match, and Phoebe will be as good as new."

Noel crowded close, his brown hair tousled and falling forward into his eyes. "Shore do. I'm a whittler and real good for a man of eight years. I can spare you a piece." He dashed outside, the door banging shut behind him.

"If y'all are done discussing me like I'm not here, I'll finish getting breakfast." Phoebe frowned. No one paid her any mind. Dismissed like a wayward child. She had half a mind to scorch the gravy.

She mixed water and milk and stirred it over a low fire. In the swirls of liquid, she envisioned Jacob Wright's face. There hadn't been a man as pretty as him on the ridge for as long as she could remember. Did the handsome face hide a man of integrity, or a scoundrel like Eli Coffman? What drove an educated man to the backwoods?

*

Rich chocolate over hot, buttered biscuits melted on Jacob's tongue. A simple luxury he hadn't enjoyed in months. The chatter of children, a warm fire, and a beautiful girl sitting opposite him. Yep Jacob got a glimpse of life if he had a family of his own. A family like the one he'd failed to keep safe. He didn't think he could do enough good in the world to make up for his past mistakes.

He speared another chunk of biscuit. He'd heard tales of the hill Folk eating strange foods. Even possum, if the situation warranted. If this was strange, he was all for it. He glanced around the table at the fresh-washed faces of the Lillie family.

Children and an old woman. Where were the parents? He'd already caused a rift with Phoebe. An ache blossomed in his chest every time she limped from the table to the stove and back. The lift would improve her ability to get around, if her pride didn't step in the way.

With the remaining piece of biscuit, he scraped his plate clean. He savored the last bite before he stood. "Let me fix that shoe, and I'll be leaving. I need four nails, a saw, sandpaper, and some blacking."

"You don't need much, do you?" Phoebe's curt tone pricked him like an ice pick. He'd overstepped his boundaries. Again.

Why was the girl pricklier than a porcupine? All he wanted to do was help her. "I'm sorry if I'm presuming anything. Do you have any of these items?"

She nodded. "The nails are in a can on the fireplace mantel. Saw's hanging on the wall in back. Sandpaper –"

"I got a piece here. The blacking too." The boy, the one they called Noel, fished a scrap from his overalls.

"Thank you." Jacob gathered the supplies, Phoebe's shoe, and headed outside. He planted himself on the top step. A frigid wind blew down the collar of his shirt.

The aroma of chocolate and butter wrapped around him. Stocking feet peeked out from under a faded skirt hem. The sight of Phoebe's shoeless state on the rough boards, her big toe poking through a hole in her socks, spurred him to hurry. Her toes must feel like cubes of ice.

Gracefully, she lowered herself onto the porch. The penetrating feel of her gaze unnerved him, like she could see right through him. His throat tightened and he mentally pushed aside the way her skin was as soft as a butterfly's wings beneath his fingers. He chose to concentrate instead on the task at hand and willed his heart rate to slow. A man with his past had no right to spend time thinking about a woman, no matter how lovely she was.

Within minutes, the entire Lillie clan surrounded him, staring with wide eyes and silent mouths as he worked. Viola pressed close to his elbow and smiled. Jacob scooted toward the porch railing. She moved closer.

He sighed. The girl's daddy would have his hands full with this one. She gobbled up every inch he created between them. Jacob was trapped by the porch rail and the hunger in Viola's eyes. How could he discourage her?

Jacob positioned the hardwood scrap over the heel of the shoe and hammered in the first nail.

Viola propped her chin in her hand, and stared at him with black button eyes. "You're smart ain't you?"

"I read a lot."

"Did you bring books with you?" Phoebe's soft question paused his hammering.

He turned. "Do you read?"

She nodded. "Whatever I can get my hands on. Books are scarce out here, so I make do with old newspapers."

"Pine Ridge has a newspaper?"

"No, but we get back issues from Compton and beyond."

"I've got a few novels." The way her face lit up at his words convinced him he'd order more as soon as funds became available.

Phoebe rose, and with the hint of a smile, backed through the doorway, somehow taking some of the early morning sun with her.

Viola smoothed the skirt of her faded rose-colored dress. "Books are a waste of time."

Jacob grinned. He now had a way of letting Viola know he wasn't interested. "I can't imagine spending time with someone who doesn't read."

She shrugged. "I could learn to like it, I reckon. For you."

JJ laughed. "Viola only likes men who pay her undying devotion and spout words of love."

The girl leaped to her feet and lunged at her brother, hands outstretched. He dashed around the corner of the building with Viola hot on his tail. The other children continued to watch Jacob as if such family spats occurred on a regular basis.

Thank you, Lord, for that narrow escape.

Finished, he got to his feet and asked Noel to

put away the tools. The boy jumped up, and scurried off. Jacob carried the shoes into the house. Had he measured correctly? Would Phoebe like the improvement? He'd buy some blacking at first opportunity to replace what he'd used.

"Try these on, please." He offered them to Phoebe.

Eyes averted, she took them and sat in the chair beside her grandmother. She slipped her feet into the scuffed shoes and stood.

Grandma eyed Jacob's work then twirled her finger in Phoebe's direction. "Walk around the room."

Phoebe strolled around the table. Her eyes widened, and she grinned. "It's a miracle. I've no limp at all."

Grandma tossed her hands up. "Praise the Lord! You ain't no teacher, Mr. Wright, but an angel sent from heaven. When my boy Ben gets home, he'll want to shake your hand."

"Glad to help." Jacob returned her grin. Finding himself compared to an angel could only be a good thing. In the past, no one considered him much more than a failure. But for this minute, this one instant, he'd believe he could be something more.

JJ burst into the cabin. "Eli's here, again." His eyes darted from Phoebe to Jacob. "Come courtin', I suppose. Got himself a handful of weeds."

Spots of color appeared on Phoebe's cheeks.

Her jaw hardened. "This won't take but a moment, Mr. Wright. Then JJ will take you to Dixon's. Thank you again for fixing my shoe. I'm much obliged." She squared her shoulders and marched outside.

Jacob peered through the open door. A wiry man stood bareheaded in faded overalls and a red and black flannel shirt at the bottom of the steps. He clutched the last of the season's wildflowers.

"I come to apologize for my behavior yesterday, Phoebe. And beg you to reconsider my offer." Eli thrust out his hand.

She took a wide stance and crossed her arms. "I've no more need of your pitying proposal, Eli. I'm no longer a cripple." She strode across the porch. "Mr. Wright, the new schoolteacher, fixed my shoe."

Cold eyes darted in Jacob's direction. "We don't take to strangers and their city ways here."

Especially when they trod on staked property, Jacob wagered. He nodded a greeting. "Just repaying the kindness of these folks." If he were a betting man, he'd also gamble that Phoebe's disability had put her right where Eli wanted her. Jacob considered himself a fair judge of character. From what he could see, Eli wanted a meek woman who obeyed his every command. And if her demeanor toward the man was any indication, Phoebe was far from being a meek sparrow.

Eli glanced from Phoebe to Jacob. The flowers fell to the ground at his feet. "Watch your back, mister." He glared at Phoebe. "Word around these here parts, Phoebe, is that your pa didn't come home last night."

Her face paled except for two bright spots high on her cheekbones. "How would folks know that?"

"There's ways. Seems he might have stuck his nose somewhere it didn't belong."

3

J acob pushed open the door to a simple wood-sided building. Outside stood a lone red and white gas pump, overhead, a painted sign that read, Dixon's Store.

"Afternoon, stranger." A portly man wearing a starched white, canvas apron strolled around the counter with his hand extended. "I'm Dixon"

Jacob clasped the offered hand and shook. "I'm Jacob Wright, the new school teacher."

"You're late."

"Got lost."

Dixon's laugh boomed across the room. "Figured as much. Hope you didn't spend the night in the cold."

"The Lillie family put me up."

"Good people." He skirted around a pickle barrel to Jacob's side of the counter.

"Could you draw me a map to the school?" Jacob leaned on the counter.

"No need. It's easy to find." The man waved his

hands in the air as he gave directions. "Go past the Lillie place. When you hit a fork, veer right. You can't miss it."

"I've seen more than one fork." And he really didn't want to get lost again.

"Yeah, but there's a big old oak there marked with the initials of folks when they started courting." Dixon cleared his throat then grinned. "Just go aways down that road until you come to the shanty. It ain't much, but a hardy young fellow like yourself ought to whip it into shape in no time."

"You over-estimate my carpentry skills." Jacob eyed bottles of cola under the glass top of a cooler. He licked his lips. Been a long time since he'd tasted his favorite drink.

"The roof don't leak in the school nor the cabin, and folks around here even stocked the place with food and wood. Make sure you let me know if you need anything else."

"You have my word on it. About my compensation—"

"Pay's ten dollars a week. First installment upon your arrival." Dixon punched a button on the register and the drawer snapped open with a *ding*. He pulled out a yellowed envelope. "We're mighty glad to have you, son. When you're ready for school to start, give a holler. And feel free to grab one of them bottles you're eyeballing."

"Thank you, I will." He used the corner of the

cooler to pop off the bottle top. "Oh, is there a church in town?"

"We got a church, but no pastor. You don't preach, do you?"

Jacob scratched his head. "I have been known to upon occasion."

He'd done a lot of everything a time or two, a lawmaker, a furniture builder, a general laborer. After his gallivanting around the country, he looked forward to this new adventure and challenge. "Give me some time to get school started. I might be able to whip up a sermon every few weeks until you get someone regular."

"Now, that's fine." Dixon's smile stretched to reveal a missing tooth. "All right, then. You're all set. Oh, wait. Since you gotta pass the Lillie's place, could you drop off this envelope?"

Jacob took the mail and shook the store owner's hand before striding outside. He nodded at two men sitting in rockers and whittling. One aimed a stream of tobacco toward a brass spittoon at their feet. From the brown stains around the spittoon, it looked like they missed more often than not. Jacob glanced down the poorly graded road, full of fist-sized rocks and potholes, toward his destination, then raised his drink to his mouth. Cola flavored carbonation poured over his tongue.

Eli Coffman leaned against a tree. "Well, if it ain't the pretty city boy." He moved to his swaybacked mule. A strand of hay hung from Eli's mouth. He tottered forward until he stood a foot from Jacob, then thrust his chin.

Jacob wiped his forearm across his wet mouth and recoiled from the pungent stench of sour whiskey on the man's breath. Hadn't Prohibition hit this far in the hills? "Afternoon, Eli."

"Glad to see you're alone, teacher. I warn't happy about you honing in on my girl."

Jacob crossed his arms. "I don't see Phoebe as being anyone's girl. She appears to be a woman with a mind of her own."

The man sagged against a post to steady. "That ain't how folks around here see it at all." He poked Jacob in the chest.

Jacob dropped his soda bottle and balled his fists. He itched to reach into his pack and pull out his gun. He couldn't. He'd sworn never to point a weapon at a human being again.

"Take care, pretty fella. Strangers don't fare well around these parts." Eli stumbled back to his mule and mounted. "I aim to marry that girl." He spat at Jacob's striped vest. "One way or the other." The other man rode away.

Maybe Jacob needed to rethink his stand on violence. He fished a handkerchief from his pocket and, with a trembling hand, wiped the spittle from his vest. If Eli made a point of provoking him again, Jacob couldn't be responsible for his actions. A man could only take so much.

He thought he'd left the threat of violence behind in the city. How did he find himself in these situations? Gritting his teeth, he stooped and picked up the shattered pieces of his drink and tossed the shards in a nearby trash can. Nodding at the two silent whittlers, he marched down the road.

Might be wise to steer clear of Eli. The man smelled like trouble. He strolled the path out of town, dropped the check off with Grandma Lillie, then continued until he stopped at a T-junction. 'Aways' up the road turned out to be more like three miles.

He caught of glimpse of Eli and mule through the tees, plodding beside the road. Jacob glared.

Eli grinned. "Hey, city slicker. Watch yore back."

The man needed to watch his own back. Jacob had done nothing, other than being new to the area, to warrant the man's malice. He shook his head and increased his pace before he did something he'd regret. Eli was too drunk to do more than shout insults, and words spewing from the mouth of a drunk failed to entice Jacob to a fight. Not anymore.

But he did need something to ride. Traveling on foot consumed too much time, and didn't seem the wisest choice with an addle-brained fool following his every move. He stared down the long, empty road stretching in the distance.

What if Eli wasn't full of whiskey the next time they both came this way? He wouldn't be able to outrun someone on a horse or a mule, even if he had decent footwear. His big toe stuck through a hole in the bottom of his shoe, and his heels sported painful blisters. Not the proper attire for a sprint through the mountains.

Tire ruts in the road showed that at least a few families owned automobiles, Jacob's primary choice of transportation. Maybe he could find one at a cheap price. He had a bit of dough stashed away.

The trees parted to reveal a small log shanty. He stopped short and gaped. A sagging lean-to provided shelter for cords of wood. Split logs served as walls. No windows broke up the small square footage. Thrusting his shoulders back and drawing in a deep breath, he entered his new abode. The first improvement would be to cut a place for a window in the front wall.

Jacob set his pack and satchel on the table. Planting his fists in the small of his back, he popped out the kinks. He pulled his father's Colt pistol from his pack and tucked it into his waistband. Maybe he should've shown it to Eli. But then again, it might have enticed the man to more violence than just angry words.

A breeze blew through the open door, fluttering an envelope on the table. He reached for it and read he'd passed the school a half-mile back. There'd been a well-worn trail forking off the road. Obviously, his idea of 'can't miss it' was different from the store owner's.

Jacob exited the cabin and headed back the way he'd come. A short walk later, he stepped into a clearing.

The schoolhouse was a twin to his cabin, right down to its lack of windows. Windows for his home moved to second on his to-do list. First, he'd have to get some light inside the schoolhouse.

Unlatching the door, he let it swing open. The sun's rays landed on dust particles in the air, highlighting them like miniature diamonds. Long sanded boards served as desks. The crowning glory was a blackboard hung on the wall. A pocked wooden table served as the teacher's desk, complete with a three-legged stool. A stack of slates sat next to a box of new chalk. Well-worn primaries lined a simple shelf. *Thank you, God.* Somebody in this poverty-stricken hollow knew the value of education.

Today was the second Monday of November, 1925. God willing, he'd start teaching in a week.

A shadow stretched across the floor.

Jacob turned and stared into the scarlet face of Eli Coffman. Jacob slowly removed the gun from his waistband and laid it on the closet desk. He straightened his shoulders and stormed toward the other man.

*

"Grandma." Phoebe hung her apron on a hook. "Can you watch the little ones? I'm going to look for Pa." Her stomach clenched. "He's never been gone for two days without saying so beforehand."

"I'd go with you if these old legs would let me." Grandma patted her thigh. "Take the shotgun."

Why should today be any different? Grandma rarely left the house unless it was for church, a quilting bee, or down to Dixon's store for a piece of horehound candy. She never traipsed the mountain. Not anymore. "I'll try to be home by supper, by dark at the latest. Did he say where he'd gone hunting?"

"Up the mountain is all he said." Grandma rocked faster, a grim look on her face. "Find my boy, child. I'll take care of the cooking today."

"Thank you." Phoebe retrieved the 22 gauge from its place behind the door. It fit in the crook of her arm like an old friend. She set off into the woods behind the house, enjoying the brisk pace her new shoe allowed. Normally, the beauty around her set a whistling tune to her lips. Today, she pushed through the thick foliage, searching for a body or a trace of someone having recently passed that way.

She kept a close watch on the sun to keep track of the time. Almost two days since Pa had left to go hunting. Did he lay dead in the hollow? Wounded on top of the mountain? Her shoulders slumped.

Where should she start looking? *Lord, guide my steps*.

Birds sang, unmindful of her fear. The trees whispered. If only they could tell their secrets, her search would be easier. From the direction of the old schoolhouse, banging cut through the autumn air.

Phoebe parted a bush. Jacob stretched to hammer a shutter over a fresh-cut window. Perspiration glistened from his bare back. The straps to his overalls hung around his hips. A puckered scar peeked above the waistband of his pants. She averted her eyes. Wouldn't do to get unseemly notions about the new schoolteacher.

She'd wondered what he'd work on first. During her learning years, she would've loved more light, instead of the gas lamps that had stung her eyes with their smoke.

"Hey, the school!" Phoebe said.

Jacob stopped and turned with a grin. "Hey, yourself. Come see what I've done." He reached for the shirt hanging on a nail.

"Opening up the front that way is a great idea." She strolled across the low grass. "Maybe I could come by tomorrow and sweep out the cobwebs for you." Heat rose to her cheeks at her boldness. "In exchange for fixing my shoe."

"No need. But I'd like the company." Jacob slid the hammer into a tab on his overalls, then slipped his arms through the sleeves of a red flannel shirt. "Where you headed?"

She swallowed the lump in her throat. "I'm looking for my pa. He should've been home by sunset yesterday." Her focus turned to the black eye and split lip Jacob sported. "What happened to you?"

"Just a tussle. Hopefully, I look better than the other guy."

"Was it Eli?" Ice gripped her heart. Jacob's newness was a threat to many of the folks living on the mountain. His life could be in danger. "He's got a hair-trigger temper. He's been known to send more than one person to the doctor."

"I held my own."

Phoebe smirked. "A dandy like you?"

"Don't let appearances fool you." Jacob pulled up his overalls.

"Fine. I'll see you tomorrow." She turned to leave.

"Wait a second. I'll go with you." Jacob closed the schoolhouse door. "You shouldn't wander by yourself."

"I've been *wandering* these woods since I could walk." Phoebe snorted. There he went again, assuming things. "You'd best stick close if you don't want to get lost."

His eyes twinkled. "Good point. I will." He bowed and waved his arm. "Lead the way."

With a toss of her head, Phoebe marched up a path that led them farther up the mountain. Words failed her at Jacob's nearness. She couldn't remember the last time she'd been alone with a man. Never one as fine looking as he was, anyway.

At a loss for words, she watched the changing colors of the leaves and listened to the breeze whisper through the branches. Jacob seemed as content not to speak as she, which reopened the door for her mind to focus on what could have befallen her pa. Her heart thumped erratically. *Please, God, don't let him be dead.*

Anything could happen to someone alone in the woods. Another hunter's wayward bullet. Moonshiners. Plain evil folk intent on harm. Wild animals. There'd been plenty of razorback hogs roaming the woods. She swiped a hand across the moisture dripping from her eyes. No way would she let any man see her break down and cry.

"Ow! Hold up." Jacob hopped on one foot, turned it up, and exposed the hole in the sole of his shoe. "I've got a thorn."

Phoebe stopped. "Your shoe's worn plumb through. You need to put cardboard inside as protection until you can get another pair."

"I don't have any." Jacob plopped on a log and plucked out a two-inch thorn. "I've been down on my luck since my last job. I've a bit of money, but I'd rather spend it on a truck."

She lowered herself beside him. "Most folks around here are short on money. Sometimes, simple things like sugar and coffee are hard to come by, but there ought to be some cardboard lying around somewhere."

"I'll make sure I always have a pot of coffee ready for you when you visit." Jacob stood and grasped her elbow to help her rise. "That's one thing I can't do without."

What made him think she'd visit? She wasn't the type to go after a man. Besides, he hadn't asked to court her. If he did, Grandma would sit silently in the corner while they made mooneyes at each other. She'd have a hissy fit if she knew they wandered the woods without a chaperone. Phoebe shrugged. Nineteen years should be past the need for a watchdog.

A coyote skittered across their path, a rabbit dangling from its mouth. Jacob jumped back and reached for his waist.

Phoebe giggled. "You act like you forgot your gun?" Here was a strong man more scared of an animal than the poor thing would be of him. "He won't bother you. Especially with both of us."

"I did forget my gun. The animal surprised me is all."

"You have a lot to learn." So the man owned a weapon. Surprising, but then, Phoebe didn't know many folks from anywhere but Pine Ridge.

"Where'd you come from, anyway?"

"Everywhere. Spent most of my childhood in Little Rock, then moseyed around, trying to find myself."

"Did you?"

"Did I what?"

"Find yourself?"

"I'm getting there. God's helping."

Phoebe sighed. She'd known her path since birth. To marry and raise a passel of kids. Not that she had anything against a woman's role in the world, but in the Hollow's eyes, she was already a spinster. Eli Coffman seemed to be her last chance at being a wife and mother.

When pigs flew. She'd raise her siblings and spend her life alone rather than marry a man with a black streak running through him.

She glanced at the lowering sun. "We'd best be heading back." Her shoulders slumped. The look on Grandma's face when she returned without her pa would tear at her insides.

"A little farther." Jacob stopped as if to listen. "I heard trucks earlier today. Came from west of my cabin. Maybe someone up there has seen your father."

"Maybe." She increased her pace, willing to grasp at any hope. Maybe Pa was passing time with some of his cronies at one of those hunting camps. He'd never done it without saying anything before, but something could've held him up.

"Here." Jacob pointed at faint tire tracks. "How many people up here have automobiles?"

"Not many." She turned in that direction. A sweet scent carried to her on the breeze. "This way."

They stepped into a clearing. Phoebe gasped. In the center, a fire blazed beneath a mash barrel. The smell of yeast filled the air. A man dozed beneath a tree, hat pulled low over his eyes. Several barrels, with drips of liquid soaking into the wood formed a line, as if waiting their turn to leave. She grabbed his hand "Back up quietly, Jacob. We have to go."

"Let me ask him a couple of questions."

"Without your gun?" She tugged harder. "Do you know what moonshiners will do if they catch us? Especially since we're here without permission?"

The clatter of a truck bouncing over ruts echoed through the trees. Lord, help them.

A muscle ticked in his jaw. "I've heard stories."

"They shoot first, and ask questions later."

4

"O kay." Jacob released Phoebe's hand and stopped at the foot of the mountain to catch his breath. "Maybe you can fly down this rock strewn path, but I can't. We're lucky I didn't break a leg."

"We can't stay here." Phoebe resumed her hold of his hand.

"I think we're far enough away not to garner attention." Jacob yanked free, straightened, and speared her with a glance. "Is your father messed up with moonshine?"

Her eyes glittered as her cheeks reddened. "He never touches the stuff."

"Maybe that pension check I dropped off yesterday isn't his only source of cash."

The force of her slap drove his head back. "How dare you? You can't come into our Hollow and start throwing words like that around. Those are fighting words." She aimed the gun at him.

Jacob lowered himself to a fallen log and gripped his hair with his hands. He'd traveled far and wide to put the temptation of drink behind him. Now, an entire still beckoned from the distance of only a few miles. *Help me, God.* "I'm sorry. If you say your father isn't making the stuff, I believe you."

But she didn't say he wasn't a middle man. He shook his head to wipe it clear of such thoughts. Most of the men around here probably knew how to get their hands on the stuff. Didn't mean they were active in the making of it.

Her lip curled, and she lowered the weapon. "It's getting dark. We'd best head home."

"Please." He rose and grabbed her arm. "I really do apologize." Seemed he did a lot of that around the prickly woman. "I want to help you find your father."

"It's none of your business. We tend to our own." Phoebe marched away, leaving him in the growing darkness of the woods. "Turn right. You'll run into your place." She tossed the directions over her shoulder.

Great. Jacob glanced around him. Alone, in a country full of bears, cougars, wolves, and makers of moonshine. He could see the headlines now. *Pine Ridge Teacher Eaten Before Opening School.* Made him wonder what happened to the teacher before him.

And how could he break through the wall built around Phoebe Lillie? This wasn't the first time he'd worked around mountain people. They had pride and a self-sufficiency that left him wanting what they had. In a few more years, the world would infringe on the people of Pine Ridge. Gone would be their idyllic simple life.

With the rest of the world struggling through a Depression, they'd soon discover the fertile soil around the Buffalo River bottoms. Would these people be able to handle their problems with a gun then?

With a glance over his shoulder, Jacob hurried home and lit the only oil lamp in the cabin. He latched the door and fell onto the cot. He'd dug himself a hole. One full of whiskey and a blue-eyed woman. He wanted to pick up his things and leave, but jobs were almost impossible to find in this day and age. Besides, the new Jacob Wright didn't quit. God sent him to this place for a purpose. He aimed to find out what it was and fulfill it. Despite the Lillie family.

He slapped the mattress with the palms of his hands. Better think of something else.

In the morning, he'd hike back to Dixon's and post a notice about school starting. Maybe try to get a list of his students so he could visit the families. And, he'd need some way of getting around. His legs wouldn't hold up on the long trails.

He folded his arms across his stomach and felt the crackle of the money. The ten dollars in his pocket seemed to be burning a hole in his pants, reminding him of something that would make his troubles seem to disappear. He threw an arm over his eyes. He'd tried that route before and lost everything.

*

Phoebe latched the cabin door behind her and glanced to where her grandma dozed in the rocking chair. After kicking off her shoes, she tip-toed to the fireplace and hung the shotgun in the rack.

"No use sneaking around. I know you're back." Grandma opened one eye. "Guess you didn't find him."

"No." Phoebe's lowered her aching body into the chair opposite the older woman.

"What did you find?"

She raised her head in surprise. "Nothing."

"Don't lie."

Phoebe sighed. "Jacob and I stumbled across an active still. About three miles up the mountain. He accused Pa of having a hand in it."

"Well, the man ain't from around here. Wouldn't know, would he?" Grandma closed her eye and leaned her head back. "Don't worry. Your Pa is a God-fearing man."

"He wants to help me look for Pa. What if he's a cover for the Feds? What if Pa *is* mixed up somehow?"

"That's a lot of ifs." Grandma resumed her

rocking. "Think on something else for a while. Like Viola's seventeenth birthday next week, or Callie's twelfth the week after. Then there's Thanksgiving. If your Pa has found himself in a peck of trouble, JJ will have to hunt the turkey."

Already? Phoebe's mouth went dry. Wasn't Grandma worried at all about her son? The woman seemed to know something Phoebe didn't and the thought wasn't reassuring. She hadn't denied the possibility of Pa having a hand in moonshine. Lots of God-fearing men did, thinking it a way to make ends meet. And most of them ended up dead.

She'd make herself crazy thinking that way. Better to concentrate on something she might be able to handle.

The younger kids all needed new shoes before the winter, and Peter's pants hung way above his ankles. Maybe she could sew a larger hem on them by using one of Pa's worn overalls. She slumped in the chair. That would just take away from Pa's clothes. None of them had extra of anything.

Why'd it all have to fall on her anyway? She loved her family but hadn't asked for the job. Now, she had to worry about that whiskey still in addition to finding out what happened to Pa. Maybe he laid dead somewhere. They might never find out.

"And not to heap more on your head, but the corn meal is running out too. Gotta take some corn to the mill to be ground tomorrow." Grandma rose.

"I'm going to bed. Starting tomorrow, the boys get the loft. My old bones can't keep climbing that ladder."

Should've made the move years ago, but the elderly woman resisted, saying she didn't have one foot in the grave yet. Tears welled and escaped, running down Phoebe's cheeks. She couldn't do this. Couldn't raise six young'uns and care for an old woman. Not without her Pa. Maybe she *should* accept Eli's offer of marriage.

The thought made her stomach acid churn. She'd send JJ to the mill tomorrow. No way did she want to face Eli who was certain to be working. Instead, she'd browse Dixon's shelves for birthday gifts and see how far she could stretch Pa's pension check.

Philippians 3:14 ran through her mind. She could do all things through Christ who strengthened her. The last year proved it. But shouldn't life offer a little fun? Some brightness once in a while to lift the burden of heavy days?

She lifted the skirt of her dress and wiped her eyes, noting how faded the fabric had gotten. Remorse flooded through her. Instead of rejoicing over the gift of newly even legs, she grumbled about things she couldn't control. To top it off, she'd been rude to the man presenting the gift. She sighed. There'd be a way of making it up to him. She'd make sure.

Their hound bayed out front, pulling Phoebe from her musing. She peeked out the hole drilled in the door. Blackness greeted her. The dog continued its noise.

Something struck the side of the house, sending Phoebe's heart into her throat. She opened the door an inch. "Boomer, come here."

The dog leaped to the porch and faced the yard. The hair on his neck bristled. A rock bounced off his ribcage, and he yelped.

Phoebe darted to the shotgun, grabbed it from its holder, and stepped onto the porch. "Who's there? Show yourself, you yellow-striped coward."

Another rock struck her in the shoulder. Pain radiated down her arm and the shotgun slipped. When the second missile missed her head by inches, she backed into the house, Boomer skittering between her legs, and slammed the door.

"What is it?" JJ burst into the room, hooking the strap of his overalls in place.

"I don't know." Phoebe handed him the gun. "Someone's throwing rocks at the house. They hit me. My arm's numb." She fell into her pa's kitchen chair.

JJ propped the shotgun beside the door and peered out. "Can't see a thing. It's as dark as the bottom of a well." He jumped back as another thud hit the house. "Good thing this old house is built solid. Best we ride it out. They'll quit sometime."

"Jacob Wright and I stumbled across a still today." Phoebe shuddered. "I wonder if Pa ran across it before he disappeared."

JJ nodded. "Flatbed trucks loaded with sugar and barrels have been going up and down the mountain all week."

"Why didn't you say something?"

"To who?"

He was right. The only law they had was each other and God's Word. Not a lot of good if moonshiners moved in. Phoebe rose and opened a drawer next to the sink. "I'm mailing a letter to Compton tomorrow. That'll get the Feds up here."

JJ stopped her hand. "No, sis. Not until we find Pa."

Her heart stuttered. "You think he's involved?"

"Don't want to, but I don't believe in coincidences. Now that you and that city teacher found the still, ain't none of us safe. We've got to pretend you didn't see anything. Keep our mouths shut. If we don't do anything, they'll leave us alone."

Phoebe nodded. Her brother made sense. If her conscience left her alone, they could continue surviving as they were. That's what the rocks were for. A warning to mind their own business.

5

Phoebe stepped on the front porch as the sun made its appearance. Ten fist-sized rocks littered the ground. Good thing she'd had the shutters closed so they didn't go through the window. Her pa would've pitched a fit if something happened to one of his glass pride and joys. Phoebe's throat swelled as she fought back the tears. If breaking a window would bring him back, she'd break one herself.

"Got the eggs." Callie handed her a basket. "Didn't get pecked once." Dimples winked from her cheeks. "Viola's almost done milking, and JJ started cutting the Timothy grass." She patted Phoebe's arm as she passed. "Don't worry. We'll make do until Pa gets home. Even the little boys can help. Noel said he'll feed the hogs, and Peter will take care of the chickens."

Phoebe blinked the moisture from her eyes. Her sister was right. She didn't have to do everything herself. The other family members were more than capable of helping. What did she feel she had to prove? She followed Callie into the house. "I think we can spare some of these eggs for breakfast. It's a good payment for everyone's hard work."

Grandma rocked in her chair and stared into the smoky embers of last night's fire. With her son's disappearance, she seemed to have aged. The lines in her face deeper, the slump of her shoulders, rounder.

"Grandma, are you all right?" Phoebe laid a hand on her shoulder.

"Just feeling life, girl. Get breakfast so you can get to the store. I'll mind the others while you're gone."

"Are you sure? I can stay home today and go tomorrow."

"Don't put off until tomorrow what you can do today." She laid her hand over Phoebe's. "I'm capable of watching things around here. Don't bury me yet."

Phoebe nodded and moved to scramble the eggs. While she worked, she went over in her mind what she'd need from Dixon's store. Pa's pension check must stretch until the next month.

They had a bit of money left from the sale of what little fruit and vegetables they didn't can for their own use, and JJ could shoot and fish well enough to keep meat on the table and hanging in the smokehouse. They'd be all right.

Normally, there was no problem having enough for the things they couldn't provide for themselves. In addition to the two gifts, they needed to buy coffee, rice, beans, flour, and fabric. Not to mention overalls. She hoped Dixon had the latest copy of the Sears Roebuck catalog.

Breakfast served, eaten, and cleaned up, Phoebe grabbed her sweater. "I'm taking the buggy." She definitely didn't want Dixon sending Eli to deliver her purchases.

"Figured you would." JJ poked his head through the doorway. "Already hitched it up."

"Thank you." Phoebe hurried outside and climbed in the simple wooden buckboard. With a flick of the reins, she set the long-legged sorrel toward Dixon's store.

Despite the autumn chill in the air, the sun caressed her head. A breeze played music in the tree branches, showering the road ahead of her with gold and crimson. A bird chattered from a nearby oak tree. The smoke from someone's fire swirled into the sky. A hawk soared overhead, diving in circles.

For a moment, Phoebe pushed the worries about her pa and the moonshine aside. She allowed the stress of feeding and clothing her siblings to lift from her shoulders. God would provide. She needed to keep reminding herself of the fact. The Bible said He remembered the sparrows. Well, the Lillie's were more than birds.

She spied Jacob Wright hiking the road and halted the buggy. "Need a ride?"

"I'm heading to Dixon's."

"Hop in." She waited until he sat then flicked the reins. "That's where I'm going."

"I'm surprised you stopped for me, considering the way we parted yesterday."

Phoebe shot him a sidelong glance. "No sense holding a grudge over a difference of opinion. That's how feuds start. Do they hold on to things in the city?"

"Pretty much." Jacob laid both arms along the back of the seat and slouched. "Thanks for the ride. All this walking can't be good for a man."

"We've a mule you can use until harvest time."

"I'm obliged."

"Once my business at Dixon's is finished, I'll give you a lift to my place and you can pick him up." It still rankled that he thought her pa was involved in moonshining, but the fact she could shove aside her feelings lifted her spirits. Phoebe convinced herself it had nothing to do with the way the sun highlighted his curls or the way his lips tilted at the corner like he kept a funny secret. Or the cleft in his chin. She wondered how her finger would fit. Or her lips. Her cheeks heated

They pulled in front of the store and Phoebe jumped out to tie the reins to the hitching post, keeping her face averted. Jacob followed her inside and pulled a flier from his pocket. Leaving him to his business, she strolled to the counter.

"Good morning, Phoebe." Dixon grinned and motioned toward her leg. "No limp."

"Mr. Wright fixed my shoe to accommodate my disability." She handed him the list and watched as he scanned the items. "I've got two dozen eggs to sell you."

"I'll give you a nickel for them. Do you want these other items on your tab?"

"No, thank you." How many times did she have to tell him they didn't like credit? "I want the twenty-five pound bags. We've need for the sacks. The girls are growing out of their clothes faster than Grandma can sew them."

While he filled her order, she browsed the items on the counter, picking up a small envelope with Kool-Aid spelled across the front. "What's this?"

"Something new. You mix it with sugar and water and have a sweet drink. Only a nickel a package."

A whole nickel? "With sugar as high as it is?" What would people think of next? She started to put the drink back, then thought of the two birthdays coming up. The fancy idea would be a special treat. "Is it as good as grape soda?"

"Some people think it's better because of the convenience. One package makes a whole quart and only uses a cup of sugar." He hefted a sack of sugar on the counter, followed by one of flour, beans, rice, then the precious coffee. "What else can I get you? Tobacco for your pa?"

"No, thanks. He's got plenty." How did Mr. Dixon not know about her pa missing, but Eli did? Phoebe decided she'd have to look further into her pa's dealings with Eli Coffman. "I need a couple of birthday presents. One for Viola, the other for Callie."

Mr. Dixon's smile widened. "And I've got a special treat for you. A new shipment of books came in yesterday."

"Really?"

"Yep. The newest in the Tarzan series and *The Great Gatsby.*"

Could she afford two? "Can you cash my pa's pension check?"

"Sure, I can. Tell me what you want, and I'll give you back what's left."

Jacob joined them at the counter. "That store-bought dress would be perfect for Viola."

Phoebe's smile faded, and she whirled to face him. "Are you sweet on my sister?"

*

Jacob stepped back. "What are you talking about?"

"Why would you pick out a dress for Viola?"

"I overheard you speaking about a gift, and knowing how prissy your sister is, thought it would be perfect." Would he ever figure these people out? Her mood changed faster than a twister in Kansas.

"Hmmph." Phoebe strolled to the rose-colored dress with a lace collar. "It would look pretty against her skin." She lifted the price tag. "$2.25! I could make one for a fourth the price."

"But not as purty." Mr. Dixon joined them. "Every girl deserves a store bought dress once in her life, and Viola's a young woman now."

"Fine. What do you have for Callie?"

"Go look in the cardboard box in the storeroom. I think you'll find something she'll like." He winked at Jacob. "You come too."

Phoebe's squeal reached them before they made it through the door. She held up a mewling calico kitten. "It's perfect. How much?"

"Free. I've no use for them, and the mama's a stray that adopted me and the missus. It'll be ready to go right around Callie's special day. Pick out a peppermint stick for each of the young'uns before you go. On the house because of your big purchase today."

"You've made my day, Mr. Dixon. And I'll take the Tarzan book."

Caught up in the excited look on Phoebe's face, Jacob dug a dollar out of his pocket. "I'll take the Gatesby, and a pound of coffee. Phoebe can borrow the book anytime she wants. We'll trade back and forth."

Her eyes hardened for a second before she nodded. The girl's prickly attitude would put a porcupine to shame. Would he ever be able to carry on a conversation with her without saying something wrong?

"Great. Let me help you load this stuff." Jacob hoisted a sack on his shoulder. "Dixon, you got any idea how many students I might have?"

"Anywhere from twenty to thirty if they all show. Most of them won't be regular, especially when snow hits. Once that happens only the ones with shoes will make it to school."

Jacob paused half-way through the door. "Has anyone contacted churches in the city to donate shoes?"

"We don't take charity, Mr. Wright." Phoebe bumped his shoulder on her way past.

Jacob shook his head. He guessed the mister in front of his last name signified he once again rubbed the woman the wrong way. He met her by the wagon. "What did I say this time?"

She lifted her chin. "A number of things. First, you buy the book thinking I can't afford it. Well, I can. I chose not to. Second, you suggest a womanly dress for my sister. You, a stranger. Third, you expect us hill folk to accept charity. We'd rather get frost bite."

"And you will with that attitude." Jacob's face heated. "In my defense, Phoebe, I didn't take into account whether you could afford the book or not. I love it when I meet someone else who enjoys reading as much as I do. Secondly, I had no ulterior motive for suggesting the dress for Viola." He ran a hand through his hair.

"I just assumed it would be something she'd like. And, thirdly, I know you don't accept charity. I've ridden the rails up and down this country, and you have got to be one of the most stubborn people I've ever met!"

"We are what we are, Mr. Wright."

"Don't *Mister* Wright, me." He tossed the sack into the wagon bed.

Phoebe glanced at his feet. "Maybe you ought to get charity to get you your own new pair of shoes." With a swish of her dress, she climbed up to the buckboard.

Jacob opened his mouth, then closed it. He'd show the little hellion. "No need, Miss Lillie." Whirling, he marched back into the store and spent another precious two dollars on a pair of ankle boots Dixon had displayed in the window. He'd be eating nothing but beans for the next week, but he'd show Miss Lillie a thing or two.

New shoes tied together and slung over his shoulder, Jacob stomped his way back to the wagon and climbed aboard. He'd regret his impulsiveness by morning, but he'd still have a new pair of shoes.

"You're as bad as what you say we are." Phoebe

laughed and urged the horse forward. "Guess you can't teach school wearing clothes as tattered as your students, can you?"

"Guess not." He crossed his arms and stared into the trees bordering the road. What was it about this woman that messed with his mind? She gripped his thoughts and actions in a tiny, calloused fist. One smile from her rosy lips could erase an angry thought, or make him stutter like a fool. And because of one smart remark, and the desire to give her a gift in a round-about-way, he held two dollars less in his pocket.

He groaned inwardly and withdrew the book from his shirt. "Here. You know why I bought it. Might as well take it now. Just let me read it when I'm ready."

"Thank you." She laughed again, the sound tinkling like a brook over stones. "We'll consider it rent for the mule."

Again, she left him speechless.

When they pulled into her yard, Jacob leaped from the wagon, wanting nothing more than to get home and away from her contradicting ways. Pretty face or not, she was a thorn in his side.

"JJ!" Phoebe hopped down. "Get the mule for Jacob."

Oh, so they were back to first names. Jacob shook his head. "What's its name?"

"We've never called it anything but Mule. He's

almost as stubborn as you."

"That's calling the kettle black." Jacob took the harness to a red-toned animal slightly smaller than a horse, then leaped onto its back. With one hand, he gripped the reins, the other his purchases.

Phoebe waved from the porch, smiling and looking prettier than a sunset. Jacob dug his heels into the mule's sides. Coming to Pine Ridge had landed him over his neck in whiskey and women. He was doomed.

6

Jacob stoked the fire in the woodstove of the schoolhouse then took a pail to fill with well water. A yawn stretched his cheeks and popped his jaws. Thoughts of Phoebe's sassiness, and the way she'd tricked him in regards to the book, kept him up thinking about her the night before. He couldn't help but wonder what it would be like to lie down with her and wake each morning with those sapphire eyes shining with love for him.

A glance at his pocket watch showed school would start in fifteen minutes. He peered down the road. Where were his students?

Back inside, he set the water on a stool and stood back to survey the room. His name scrawled across the blackboard. The pile of slates sat within easy reach and warmth from the stove cut the morning's chill. His new shoes pinched his feet but couldn't dispel the sense of joy flooding through him. The sound of voices outside magnified the emotion, and Jacob turned to welcome the children.

A scowling JJ led the way for Callie, Noel, and Peter. Jacob smiled wider. Obviously the boy wasn't excited about schooling at his age. Way to go, Phoebe.

"What happened to your face?" JJ squeezed past him.

Jacob put a hand to his cheek. The bruises should've faded by now. He'd glanced in the mirror. Just a trace of yellow below his eye.

Laughing, a mixed group of boys and girls pushed and shoved their way to the school house. Jacob counted twenty-five students from the ages of six to the mid-teen years. He took a deep breath and rang the cowbell hanging beside the door.

"Morn'in, teacher," was tossed his way as the students filed past and hung coats and lunch pails on nails pounded into the wall. They chose seats by age, youngest in front, oldest in back.

Someone had taught them well. He strode to the front of the room and turned to face the class. "Good morning. My name is Jacob Wright. I expect to be addressed as Mr. Wright." He winked at the Lillie children. "And I am looking forward to a great school year."

The day passed in a flurry of getting acquainted and finding where the children were in regards to their studies. Overall, their amount of schooling amazed and pleased Jacob. He stopped JJ at the end of the day. "Who taught before me?"

JJ lowered his head. "My ma, afore she died did some, and Phoebe a while after that. Before them, we had a man, but he got killed by a feller who made mule whiskey." He raised his eyes. "Best you take care, Mr. Wright. I know Phoebe's got you wanting to help her find out what happened to Pa, but some folks in these hills don't take to strangers at all. Not even if they are trying to help by giving their children an education."

"Thanks for the information." Jacob swallowed past the lump in his throat. What in the world was mule whiskey?

The boy stepped off the stoop and turned. "By the way, the circuit preacher is in town, and there'll be a cake bid after church." He grinned. "You might want to bid on Phoebe's. She'll have the carrot cake."

Jacob laughed. "Thanks for the tip."

"Oh, and Grandma said to make sure you come next week for Thanksgiving. She wants me to offer before anyone else. I'll be going out to get a turkey this weekend." His smile faded. "There ain't no school that week is there?"

"No, we'll have a break. Tell your grandma I'd be happy to come."

"Friday is Viola's birthday. You ought to come to that, too."

Jacob didn't want to encourage the girl. "I'll think on it."

Once the students left, Jacob sat behind his desk and gazed over the empty room. A successful day. He gave the glory to God, and prayed the majority of the students would be consistent in coming. He wasn't naïve enough to believe they'd come during planting or harvesting. That left only a few months to crowd in as much teaching as possible.

He planted his hands flat on the desk and pushed to his feet. Tomorrow was another day. He'd make school as exciting as possible to encourage the children to return. He smiled. A Christmas program would be just the thing to get the kids and their families involved.

*

Phoebe sat beside the trundle sewing machine converting one of Callie's old dresses into something the fast growing Maggie could wear. She'd been delighted to find a catalog stuffed in among her purchases and ordered both little boys new overalls. They could wear the ones she ordered to school and save the old ones for play and work.

Beside the fireplace, Grandma's knitting needles clacked, providing background music to the whir of the machine. The socks she made would keep their feet warm during the winter months. Canned goods lined the shelves in the pantry, meat hung in the smokehouse, and potatoes nestled in the dirt and straw below the house. If not for the uncertainty of her pa's fate, Phoebe would count herself a lucky girl.

"What do you think about that teacher fellow?" Grandma's question caused Phoebe to press hard on the trundle, sending the fabric off to the side.

She sighed and prepared to rip out the stitches. "What?"

"Jacob Wright. What do you think about him?"

"Don't think about him much. He's nice enough. The kids like him." Phoebe bit the thread.

"Purty, ain't he?"

Phoebe spun on her stool. "What are you trying to get at, Grandma?"

"There's two girls of marrying age beneath this roof. I aim to snag him for one of them."

"Don't we have a say in the matter?" Jacob's curls and emerald eyes shone before her eyes. Although she didn't believe she had time for a husband and family, not with the load of responsibilities she carried, Phoebe knew she wouldn't be able to handle Viola winning the man's heart.

"Don't need to. Young people don't have a lot of sense anyway." Grandma cackled. "I'm going to help Viola bake a cake for Sunday. Maybe pretty boy will bid on hers. She's turning seventeen. Plenty old enough to keep time with a fellow."

Phoebe raised her eyebrows. Unfortunately, Viola'd been "keeping" time with fellows since she was fourteen. What would Grandma and Pa think if they knew of Viola's flirtatious ways? Pa'd probably whip the skin right off her legs. Phoebe turned back to her job. Nope, she didn't want her loosy-goosey of a sister winning over Jacob Wright.

When the setting sun made sewing difficult, Phoebe rose and headed outside to bring in some meat for a stew. She reached into the smokehouse and grabbed some pork fat, then latched the door closed against the animals.

Something rustled in the brush. Phoebe whirled and clutched the meat to her chest. "Who's there?"

"It's the widow Williams." A thin woman in a faded and patched dress stepped from the bushes. "I was hoping to see your pa."

"I haven't seen him in a week."

The woman sagged against a tree. "He went hunting then stopped by my place to drop off one of the two rabbits he'd killed. Then said he had to be getting home to you young'uns. It pains me to know he didn't make it."

"What do you know?" Phoebe gripped her arm.

"I saw Ben's face in my mirror this morning." Tears ran down her face. "You know what that means. Something bad must've happened. You come by my place tomorrow. I'll show you what I know."

"What's your name?" Although Phoebe worked hard at tossing the old superstitions aside, the widow's speaking of foreboding sent a shiver down

Phoebe's spine.

"Nancy." She melted into the shadows. "You come see me."

The evening chill alerted Phoebe to the fact she stood without a sweater in the deepening dusk. After last night's hail of rocks, she didn't want to be outside after dark. With another glance around her, she dashed for the house and burst inside. The faces of her family stared at her.

"Uh, I heard something."

"Haunts, I reckon." Grandma pushed to her feet. "No moon tonight. There's bound to be a few wandering around. Dead things can't hurt you. It's the living you got to worry about."

Ghosts. Phoebe shook her head. Of course, Nancy Williams *had* resembled a specter with her pale skin and flyaway hair. Was her pa courting the widow? Didn't she have a load of children herself? Phoebe shrugged. If he married again, her load would be lightened, and she could find out God's plan for her life. There had to be more than mothering her siblings. The thought made her more determined to find out what happened to her pa.

She'd assign more chores to lazy Viola, thus giving herself time to search the mountain more thoroughly. Phoebe glared at her sister. If it became a competition between the two of them for the attention of Jacob Wright, would the man want a decorative woman, or someone useful? She shook her head. There wasn't time for fanciful dreaming.

"JJ, can you step outside for a minute?" Phoebe motioned toward the door then stepped onto the porch. When her brother joined her, she moved to the small square of light spilling from the window. "The Widow Williams spoke to me. She was hiding in the bushes when I went to the smokehouse."

"So? Pa's been keeping company with her for a few months now."

"Why didn't I know?"

"You're always too busy. You never have any fun since Ma died." JJ hooked his thumbs in the straps of his overalls. "Did she say where Pa is?"

Phoebe shook her head. "Doesn't know. Thought he'd come home. She wants me to go up to her place tomorrow. Said she's got something important to show me."

So do I. I got tired of waiting for Pa to come home so I busted the lock on his shed with a rock." JJ took Phoebe's arm. "Come see what I found. You ain't gonna like it."

Her heart leaped into her throat, and her hands chilled as she followed her brother behind the house. Her pa's shed sat back against the tree line making Phoebe wish she'd brought a lantern. "It's too dark to see anything."

JJ lit a candle he picked up from the ground. "I stuck this here earlier today." He lit the stub with a match from his pocket then held it high as he swung the door open.

Phoebe peered inside and gasped. Sacks of sugar lined the walls and were piled as high as the roof. Glass jars of clear liquid lined a shelf over her head. A sawed off shotgun lay on top of one of the sugar stacks. She hadn't known her father possessed a hog leg, much less kept it in a shed.

Tears welled in her eyes. In front of her was all the proof she needed that her father was involved in moonshine. If he didn't make it, he supplied or sold it. All the times he told her he never touched the stuff had been lies. She slammed the door shut.

"What do we do with all this? We can't let anyone know." If Jacob found out, he'd want nothing more to do with them.

"I'm taking the hog's leg. If whiskey runners got Pa, they might be coming here next. Especially if they find out we have a fortune in sugar stashed on our property. Not to mention jars of the stuff."

Phoebe sagged against the side of the building. "There's more here than we're seeing. Most of the people on this mountain keep a jar or two for medicinal purposes. Nothing seems wrong with that. That sheriff from Compton shows up here once a month, nosing around. He's even taken a sip with Pa. You don't think Pa has a still stashed away somewhere, do you? Or that the Sheriff's playing both sides of the fence?"

"I don't see how Pa'd have the time. Not with

the hours he spends in the fields. I can't speak for the Sheriff." JJ shook his head. "No, Pa's either holding this for someone else, or he stole it."

Phoebe's blood ran cold. "Stole it?" Not her pa. The man who'd held her as a baby. The God-fearing person who shunned wrong and embraced right. He'd taken very seriously the scripture stating to raise up a child in the way they should go. "I don't believe it. Something else is happening here."

JJ raised an eyebrow. "The evidence speaks for itself."

"You're reading it wrong." Phoebe chewed the inside of her cheek. Pa wouldn't steal or make moonshine. Not if he could help it.

Unless it meant life or death for someone.

7

A rooster crowed. Phoebe glanced at the window. Barely daybreak. She lay in the bed beside her sister and stared through the dawn toward the ceiling. Thoughts of her father mixed up in moonshining chilled her blood. Even on the mountain, they'd heard of prohibition. She'd read stories in the out-dated newspapers of gunfights and people dying over an imagined wrong. She'd witnessed her share of deaths over something as simple as trespassing. Most of the people she knew had stills to make their own drink, none of the scale of what she now suspected was happening in Pine Ridge. Should she send for the sheriff?

Jacob came from the city. She'd ask him tomorrow. Hopefully, he'd have some words of wisdom to calm her spirit. A smile crossed her face as she pictured him with his Colt tucked into his pants. Just in case, he'd said.

Phoebe rolled out of bed groaning. She elbowed

Viola. "Get up. Chores are waiting."

"They're always waiting." Her sister pulled the quilt over her head.

"Tell me something I don't know." Phoebe yanked the cover off her, dropped it on the floor, and then marched to where her day dress hung. She donned her clothes, tossed another warning to get out of bed over her shoulder and made her way to the kitchen.

Grandma fried bacon over the stove. "JJ told me what you found." She turned and waved her spatula. "Danger is coming, Phoebe. Mind your steps."

"Do you think Pa is dead?" She plopped onto a chair.

"No, I don't. I'd feel it in my bones if he was. I might feel a lot of things, but that ain't one of them."

Phoebe glanced at her folded hands. "I'm going to visit the Widow Williams today. She's got something to show me."

"Hmmph." Grandma turned back to her cooking. "Looks like we'll be adding her three kids to ours one day. I hope to have you or Viola married off by that time or this cabin will burst at the seams."

Goodness. She remained fixated on having one of them marry Jacob Wright. Phoebe took a deep breath. She wouldn't be able to bear it if the man chose her sister. Another blow from life. One she wouldn't get over. She squared her shoulders. Well, she wouldn't primp or act unseemly in order to win his favor. He'd have to love her as she was. Thorns and all.

Why did everyone seem to know about her pa courting besides her? Had she been so wrapped up in self-pity to notice what went on with her family? Selfish, that's what she was. That attitude would stop now. She'd do what God required of her and be content doing so.

"JJ said Mr. Wright would join us for Thanksgiving. If you hurry, you might have time to make yourself a new dress. Viola will have that pink one you bought her. Can't let the girl show you up. You gotta give her a run for her money." Grandma set the bacon on the table. "Blue looks real purty on you. I've got some fabric in the cabinet. I was going to make my burying clothes with it, but I want you to have it. I've decided to wear green when I'm dead."

Wonderful. An outfit made from something planned for burial. Phoebe sighed as her siblings rushed to join them at the table. One more thing to do. Grandma wouldn't quit until the dress was made. She'd glance through the catalog and copy one of the gowns in there. It'd be every bit as fashionable as Viola's birthday gift. Despite her misgivings over Grandma's donation, a piece of the wall around Phoebe's heart cracked.

"Oh, and be practicing on the Dulcimer. I want Mr. Wright to hear your voice. Like an angel it is." Grandma gave Phoebe a wink.

"I can sing." Viola pouted, joining them.

"Like a hound dog." JJ laughed, eliciting a glare from his sister.

"I don't sing for strangers, Grandma." Phoebe scooped eggs onto her plate. "You know that."

"He ain't a stranger."

"He's not family." Phoebe forked food into her mouth, aware of the fact she wished he were, as long as he came as her husband. She sighed. Dreaming about a handsome face wouldn't get her work done. She finished eating and pushed her plate aside. "Viola, do the dishes. I'll be home in a bit."

"I'm getting tired of you bossing me around like I'm a child."

Phoebe shrugged. "Then start doing a woman's share of the work." She glanced around the table at the younger children. "Y'all better hurry and get to school." She slung her sweater around her shoulders, grabbed the shotgun, and then stormed out of the house.

God, I'm sorry. But times are hard, and I'm worn out from worrying about Pa.

She felt like an old woman, aching in the bones and weary in her spirit. Thank God, the preacher would be in the hollow on Sunday. She needed uplifting and a time of fellowship.

The widow's log cabin sat back from the road, surrounded by weeds and thick brush. A three-legged dog brayed from the end of a tattered rope as Phoebe made her way to the porch. The front door swung open before she could knock.

"Come in. Quickly." Nancy stepped back.

Phoebe stepped into the dim recesses of a tiny but clean home. Three big-eyed children under the age of ten stared from their seats at the table. A bowl of oatmeal sat in front of each of them.

"Come into the back room." Nancy grasped Phoebe's arm and dragged her with her. She shut the door to the bedroom then pulled a cardboard box from beneath her bed. "Your pa left this with me in case anything happened to him. I haven't opened it. He said to give it to you."

Phoebe took the box. "Is my pa making or selling whiskey?"

"No more than the other man. He told me he wanted to put a stop to the whisky running going on here. Said it's reaching massive proportions." Nancy twisted her apron. "I'm afraid they found out what he's up to."

"What do you mean?" Phoebe's knees weakened, and she sat on the bed.

"Your pa was going to become one of them and sabotage their dealings." Tears welled in the woman's eyes. "I'm afraid they discovered him."

"Thank you." Phoebe rose. Her stomach

recoiled. "If you find out anything, please send word."

"I will."

Instead of going home, Phoebe headed toward the schoolhouse. She sat on a stump a few yards from the building and opened the box. She unfolded a list of names from around a key. A gasp escaped her as she read Eli Coffman and the sheriff's name among five others. Were these the men making illegal brew, or were they allies of her father? What would they do if they couldn't trust the law?

She gazed around the peaceful yard. From the position of the sun, it'd be lunchtime soon, and the quiet would be disrupted by childish games. A plan that turned her stomach formed in her mind. If successful, she might find out what happened to her father. But she might lose any chance at winning the heart of Jacob Wright.

*

Jacob followed his students outside for recess and spotted Phoebe sitting beneath a tree. His breath caught at the vision she made. The sun shone on her hair, highlighting the gold with streaks of white. Autumn leaves in colors of scarlet, pumpkin, and gold rained around her. He gazed a moment more to fix the image in his mind then made his way to her side.

She closed the box in her lap and raised shadowed eyes. "Jacob."

"Were you expecting someone else?" He grinned and sat beside her. "Is there something I can do for you?"

Her shoulders slumped. "I'm afraid not."

"Let me help." Jacob placed a hand over hers. "I want to."

"People will think we're courting, and I can't let that happen." She bowed her head, allowing her hair to fall forward.

"Why not? I'd like the honor." He tilted his head trying to see her face.

Her sigh seemed to carry the weight of the world. She glanced toward the play yard where the children screamed in a game of tag. "I've found out my father *is* involved in moonshine. If he never returns home, I've a family to raise."

"Any man you marry will gladly shoulder that burden with you." What was she trying to say? Jacob leaned against the tree trunk and crossed his arms. She wasn't turning him down because of a sense of duty. Something else ran through her pretty head. She wouldn't get rid of him that easy. He wasn't as shocked as he thought he'd be by her declaration of her pa's dealings. Deep down, he'd already suspected as much.

"Are you proposing marriage, Mr. Wright?" She stiffened, her eyes wide.

Was he? He'd only known the woman a week, yet seemed to know everything he wanted to about her. Her strength wasn't like anything he'd ever seen before. Whatever life dished out, Phoebe would handle with squared jaw and a stiff spine. A love of family rose above her beauty and made her shine like the brightest star in the heavens. It wouldn't be hard to imagine Phoebe as Mrs. Wright. "Is the idea awful to you?"

"You're a handsome man. Any woman would be honored to be seen hanging on your arm."

"Any woman but you, you mean. Why don't you tell me what's on your mind? I'm sure I can help. I've got a good head on my shoulders. If not me, then God. His Word says to 'cast our cares upon Him, for His burden is light."

"I'm familiar with the scripture. The people on this mountain aren't completely ignorant."

"I didn't mean to imply—"

"I'm sorry. I'm tired, is all."

JJ dashed to their side. "Recess is about over, Mr. Wright. Can I ring the bell?"

"Sure." Jacob frowned. They'd resolved nothing. He hated to leave her without getting to the bottom of her troubles. "Wait for me when school is finished. Let me walk you home."

She shook her head and rose. "I've decided to accept Eli Coffman's proposal. After a respectable period of courtship, of course. You and I can't be anything other than friends. It'd be best if you set your sights on Viola." With a tilt of her chin, she marched down the road. But not before he saw the beginning of her tears.

Fine, Miss Phoebe Lillie. Pretend you don't care. He knew different. Just as he knew he'd change her mind before a marriage to anyone but him could take place. If the woman wanted courting, then courting she would get. Hot enough to knock her stockings into the next county. And he'd find her father to boot. Dead or alive.

The cowbell rang across the clearing and Jacob followed the students inside. Concentration flew out the window as he tried listening to the younger students read out loud. Especially when he spotted Eli standing outside the window. Thank the Lord, Phoebe had headed home.

Eli stepped inside the moment everyone rose to leave. He waited, a grin beneath his straggly beard until Eli acknowledged him.

"Eli."

"Teacher."

Jacob turned to erase the blackboard. When the man didn't speak, he turned back to face him. "I'm busy. Is there something I can help you with?"

"Wanted to deliver the news myself." He hooked his thumbs into his overalls and rocked on the balls of his feet.

"What news is that?"

"About me and Phoebe getting engaged. It'll be all over the mountain by morning."

Jacob's hand stilled. The woman worked fast, he'd give her that. He turned and speared the other man with his gaze. "I don't aim to give up that easily, Eli. Now, I don't figure you for a man that runs from a fight. Especially considering we both still carry bruises from the other one."

"You want to come to fisticuffs over this?" He stopped rocking.

"No. I'm just saying, may the best man win." Jacob set the eraser on the sill and extended his hand.

Eli's grin widened.

8

Jacob stood on Phoebe's front porch clutching a bouquet of autumn flowers in one hand and a wrapped bottle of rose-scented toilet water perfume in the other. He'd spotted Eli's mule tied outside and prepared himself for an evening of battle with the man. He patted the butt of his pistol, then knocked on the door.

"Good evening, Jacob." Viola opened the door and cocked a hip.

"Happy Birthday, Viola." Jacob handed her the gift. "You look lovely."

She twirled. "Phoebe mentioned you picked it out. Doesn't the birthday girl get a kiss?" Viola puckered her lips.

Jacob lifted her hand and brushed his lips across the soft skin. No sense in encouraging her. He'd met her type more times than he could count.

The girl winked and sashayed ahead of him into the house. "I hope you like chocolate cake."

"My favorite." He nodded to Eli who sat in a

chair beside the fire then made his way to Phoebe's side. "These are for you." He placed a kiss on a cheek softer than a flower petal. "Although they don't compare to your beauty."

She blushed and paused in her sprinkling of sugar on top of the cake. "You shouldn't have." She cast a nervous glance toward Eli. He frowned. Viola's eyes cast daggers.

Grandma's gaze flicked between them from the comfort of her rocking chair, her wise eyes seeming to miss nothing. Her lips tilted at the corners. She clearly enjoyed the interaction between the sisters and the men vying for Phoebe's hand.

"Don't worry about Eli." Eli grabbed a mason jar from the shelf above the sink. "All's fair in love and war, they say. The two of us have an understanding." After placing the flowers in water, he turned and leaned against the counter. "Did Eli bring you anything?"

"Shhh." She carried the cake and placed it in the center of the table. "Would you step outside with me, please?"

Jacob shot a grin toward the glowering Eli. "I'd be happy too." Maybe wooing Phoebe would be easier than he thought.

Once they stepped on the porch and closed the door, Phoebe whirled. If she could spit venom, she most likely would have. Her eyes turned the color of ice. Scarlet spots of color sat high on her cheeks.

"What are you doing?"

"A simple competition for your hand." He crossed his arms.

She planted fists on her hips. "I don't want your attention!"

"I beg to differ." Jacob took one of her hands in his. Her eyes warmed into spring lakes he could drown in. He focused on lips the shade of cherries and wondered what if would feel like to kiss her. "What are you afraid of? That I might win?"

"No."

"Is that a new dress? It's a good color for you."

"Stop it. You'll ruin everything." She yanked free. "Oh, never mind." Phoebe stormed into the house.

Her words confirmed she had something up her cornflower-blue sleeve. Had she made the new dress to impress him or Eli? Either way, she looked more beautiful than a summer day, and he intended to enjoy her company. He squared his shoulders and reentered the house.

Phoebe sat in a chair beside Eli, a polished Dulcimer on her lap. Her hand held a hawk feather. She took a deep breath and began to play, her voice melding with the music. Angels couldn't have sounded sweeter. When she raised misty eyes to Jacob's, his legs weakened, and he sat at the table.

O hush you lest you break my heart

She sang straight to his soul. A cry for help, it

seemed. *Lord, why must she be so stubborn?*

Ten thousand loves have already parted

By the time she finished there wasn't a dry eye in the room. Except for maybe Eli who gazed at her with an attitude of ownership.

"Beautiful, child." Grandma dabbed her face.

"My turn." Viola stood in front of the fireplace and folded her hands before screeching out the verses to 'O Susanna'.

Jacob clinched his jaw. She might have a pretty face, but only a wounded cat would like her singing. Toddler Maggie clamped her hands over her ear, causing Jacob to bend and fiddle with his shoe to hide the urge to laugh. When Viola finished, he clapped along with the others and uttered a silent prayer of thanksgiving that she was finished.

Phoebe smiled at her sister. "Time to cut the cake."

"I'll help." Jacob leaped to his feet.

Eli crossed his arms. "Woman's work, city boy. If you want to win a woman's heart, learn your role in things."

"You do things your way, and I'll do them mine."

"Good luck." Eli guffawed and clapped him on the shoulder.

Fine by him. Eli's heavy-handed ways wouldn't win Phoebe's heart. If Jacob was a betting man, he'd lay money on it. The woman wanted to be courted, cherished, loved. All he'd ever seen on her face was the ghost of a smile. He'd get her to lay her troubles aside one day and laugh loud enough to be heard in the next county.

*

Phoebe glared at the two men resembling roosters squaring off in a yard full of hens. Couldn't Jacob see he'd already won her heart but she couldn't accept the gift of love he offered? Not until she found out what happened to Pa? Should she explain to him? Would he wait for her?

She shook her head to clear it of the questions rattling around inside. The look on his face told her he knew the song she'd sung had been meant for him. She tossed the rag she washed dishes with into the sink, splattering her new dress with dish soap. She'd take out the garbage. That would clear her head.

"I'll do that." Jacob reached to take the trash can from her hand.

"No, that's okay. I need some fresh air to clear my head."

"Are you sure?" His eyes searched hers.

"Let the woman do her work, city boy." Eli lit a cigar.

Phoebe rolled her eyes, ignoring the heated look from Viola. It would anger the girl to have the attention off her and on Phoebe. If she left, the men would have no choice but to pay attention to the birthday girl instead of strutting around for a favorable look from Phoebe. "I'll be back in a minute."

An idiot. That's what she was. Playing with Eli's affections could only guarantee trouble. He'd argued her request for a time of courtship, but the thought of being alone with the man made her nauseous. Not to mention the trickle of fear that ran down her spine when he looked at her. There was something off about the man. Phoebe pushed open the back door and stepped outside.

The dark of night welcomed her. Bullfrogs serenaded with the sound of evening insects as background music. With no one to see, she grinned and skipped down the stairs toward the steel drum they used to burn their garbage in. Alone, the world didn't hold as many burdens, and Phoebe could allow herself a moment of joy.

"Phoebe."

She froze as her heart shot to her throat. "Pa?"

Her father stepped from the shadows. The stock of a sawed-off shotgun showed beneath the bib of his overalls. "I've heard some disturbing news, daughter."

She threw herself into his arms. "Where have you been? I've been beside myself with worry."

Ben Lillie grasped her arm and pulled her into the shade of the trees. "You can't tell anyone what I'm doing. Not even Grandma. Tell her I'm stringing wire for the REA. Anything."

The Rural Electrification Administration hadn't moved this far north. "She might believe it." She peered through the dark at his face. "She's making herself sick."

"There's evil moving, Phoebe. A darkness I don't want my family involved in. Especially the young'uns. You know how hard headed JJ is." He placed his hands on her shoulders. "What's this I hear about you accepting Eli Coffman's proposal? The man's dangerous."

"Is that why his name is on that list you gave the Widow Williams?" That meant the sheriff was involved too. Phoebe's blood ran cold.

Her pa shook her. "Mind me, girl. Stay away from him."

"I can't. I want to help you. You know I can. Pa, you're involved in moonshine. JJ and I found the stash of corn and sugar. I can pretend as well as you. Lots of folks make the stuff for extra money. They'll think the same of us." He had to believe her. "You can't take on something this big by yourself. I'll send for the Feds if you don't let me help."

"No. It's too early for that." He released her. "You got anyone that can look out for you? Someone that can be trusted to keep their mouth shut?"

"Are you accepting my help?"

"Yes, God help me, I am."

She nodded. "The new school teacher can be trusted. I like him, Pa. And I think he feels the same about me."

He drew her into his arms, smelling of whiskey and tobacco. "That's fine, Phoebe. Real fine." He tightened his hold. "Just remember not to believe all the stories you'll hear about me."

"I couldn't." Tears coursed down her cheeks.

"Be careful with Eli. I realize what you're trying to do, but you're playing with fire."

"I'll take care."

"You know that oak that's been sawed in half, leaving the inside empty?

She nodded.

"I'll leave you messages there. Check every day, okay? If you don't hear from me for two days straight, call in the Feds. That means I'm most likely dead, and our cover's been blown. My turn at watching the still will be over soon, and I'll be able to come home for a few days. I'll be there for turkey day." He kissed the top of her head, released her, and then melted into the woods.

The urgency in her pa's voice kept the fear pulsing through Phoebe's veins. At the same time, relief flooded her that he still lived. She turned back to the house. Jacob's silhouette appeared in the lit back door. *Would* he help her? She'd find a way of asking after she got rid of Eli.

"I need to talk to you." She squeezed past Jacob

into the house. "In a bit. It's important."

She stopped in front of Eli. "It's time to go. I'll walk you out."

He frowned. "Kind of early, ain't it?"

"I'm worn out from the cooking and baking, and you're children are waiting on you. Your daughter's barely old enough to care for herself much less her siblings." She forced a smile to her lips. "I'll see you tomorrow."

He rose and kissed her cheek. Phoebe fought not to shrink back, instead enduring the scratch of his whiskers and the stench of his cigar-scented breath. Once he'd left, she nodded at Jacob and headed again to the back of the house. She took a deep breath, folded her hands, and began.

"My pa spoke to me when I was out here earlier. He's fine, but involved in something dangerous. I aim to help him." She lifted her chin and focused on the shadows of Jacob's face. "Eli is involved somchow. That's why I'm allowing his attention. I need to gain his trust."

Jacob grinned. "I thought it was something like that."

"I'm asking for your help, Jacob. The only way my pa will let me assist him, is if there is someone I can trust to look out for me."

It warmed her heart that he didn't hesitate to help in any way she needed. Had God ever made a finer man than Jacob Wright?

"I'll help in whatever way you see fit. But the idea makes me nervous. With me and Eli both courting you, I'll be around the same as him. What, exactly, is your father trying to do?"

Phoebe shrugged. "Take down a passel of moonshiners single-handedly, it looks like."

9

The ground sparkled with ice. The last of the leaves lay withered and dry beneath the crust. Phoebe took a deep breath; the air cutting in its coldness. She pulled a tattered wool coat around her and stomped to where JJ and the rest of the family waited in the wagon.

Viola proudly held a lopsided chocolate cake in her lap while Grandma cradled Phoebe's famed carrot one. The smile hadn't left her face since Phoebe told her about Pa working for the REA. Grandma seemed to think money would no longer be hard to get. That, with the coming of electricity, came the means to riches. How would she respond when she found out it was a lie?

Phoebe shuddered from more than the cold. The dreaded cake and pie sell-off was after church. Having to eat lunch with whatever man bought your baked goods seemed ridiculous to her. She shrugged. The money would go toward buying new hymn books for the church. She didn't want to be a hindrance to a worthy cause.

She cast a glance at the darkening sky, and thanked God the bake-off would be held in the Tuckers' barn. Her leg ached when chilled and today's temperature went straight to the bone. There'd be snow before the day was through, and JJ would be hunting their Thanksgiving turkey in it tomorrow.

Climbing onto the buckboard, she flicked the reins and wished for an automobile. She'd never ridden in one, but the pictures she'd seen made them look warmer than a horse-drawn wagon, and a smoother ride besides. She clicked her tongue and they clopped the five miles to church. The sight of Jacob and Eli waiting in front of the white building, made her want to keep moving.

Grandma laughed. "Those two are making spectacles of themselves. Pick one and put them out of their misery. I'll help you when we get home. We'll write their names on slips of paper and stuff them in your bodice. You'll dream of your future husband tonight. I guarantee it."

She already did without the benefit of superstition. It was Jacob's face that filled her thoughts while sleeping.

Viola scoffed. "I don't know why they're focusing on Phoebe. I'm prettier than she is."

"Depends on who's doing the looking. Anyway, pretty is as pretty does." Grandma handed Phoebe her cake then waited for JJ to help her down. "Careful or folks might see deep inside you and see things you don't want them to."

Viola narrowed her eyes at Phoebe then waited for JJ to turn to her. Grandma rushed off to tell her friends about her son getting a job with the REA. Phoebe cringed. Folks would expect to see electrical wires before long, and her pa would have to come up with another falsehood to cover his tracks.

It didn't take long for most of the eligible young men of the hollow to swarm around Viola once her feet hit the ground. Her giggle drifted across the cold air on wisps of smoky exhalation when she breathed.

Phoebe sighed and glanced back to where the two men competing for her hand stood. Jacob dashed forward and took the cake from her hands, trying to peek beneath the lid. She slapped his hands away. "You aren't supposed to know which one is mine."

He leaned closer. "What if I say your Grandma told me?"

"Then you'd better come up with a plan to keep Eli from buying it. He's probably got more money laying around than you do." She flashed him a smile over her shoulder and strode into the building. He'd cared enough to find out what kind of cake she'd brought. *Oh, please, Lord, let Jacob be the one to buy it.*

The temperature inside the church rose several degrees as the parishioners crowded inside. Several people exclaimed over Phoebe's lack of a limp, and her face heated. The burn continued as Jacob and Eli sat on each side of her on the polished wooden pew. Several sets of eyes glanced in their direction. Women's eyebrows rose. Men snickered behind beards or moustaches. Phoebe crossed her arms and slouched.

They rose, sang some hymns, and then sat again. Eli's and Jacob's closeness made Phoebe claustrophobic. She struggled to concentrate on the pastor's words of thanksgiving, even during the difficult times the hollow would face during the years of the Depression.

She *was* grateful. For a lot of things. The ability to walk without a limp, her father being alive, Jacob's attention, food on the table, and a few dollars stashed in a mason jar under the porch. But the fear and worry over what she'd volunteered to do to help her father cast a shadow over the brightness of her blessings.

Life always seemed to hold something better right out of her reach. Like a carrot dangled in front of horse. She didn't want a big fancy house or a life of lying around pampering herself, but some easing of burdens would be nice. Maybe she should stop reading so many books. They filled her head with things she couldn't have.

Her gaze flicked to Jacob's strong profile. There were things close at hand that were every bit as wonderful. A man as handsome and romantic as what a girl could find between the pages of a book. She glanced at Eli and stifled a giggle. And a villain as nasty.

He caught her looking and scowled. "Pay attention to the sermon. You're a grown woman, Phoebe. Not a squirmy child."

A man worried about behavior in a church building that made a living running moonshine. Who would've thought? Phoebe forced a smile to her face and lowered her eyes.

Jacob nudged her knee with his, brightening Phoebe's spirits. Although secret, their mutual fondness lit her world with a ray of sunshine brighter than any star that burned over the mountain. She'd chosen who she wanted for a husband. His name was Jacob.

*

The women's pies and cakes spread across a table-cloth covered plank of wood set across sawhorses. Flavors of every type enticed the single men to lay down their hard-earned money for the opportunity to have lunch with a pretty girl. If he hadn't been told a head of time, Jacob wouldn't have known which cake to pick.

It would've been easy to pick Viola's. Every man in the place seemed to know which was hers, and crowded around that end of the table. Jacob stood off to one side, not wanting to point to Eli which one was Phoebe's. He should've thought to tell her to make a fallen, bad tasting one. Then he'd be the only bidder.

The pastor stepped behind the table and pointed at the first item for bid. A double-layer vanilla. Jacob bid ten cents. Eli bid twenty. Jacob smiled and waited for the next one.

As the game progressed, Jacob's smile grew wider and Eli's face redder. Jacob's pockets lightened, along with the other man's, and he prayed he'd whittled Eli down enough that he could win the bid on Phoebe's concoction. He checked his money. Two dollars. It would have to be enough. Only two cakes remained.

The pastor moved to Phoebe's cake. Jacob glanced at Eli and grinned. Eli yelled twenty-five cents.

"Thirty." Jacob raised his hand.

"Forty."

"Fifty." Jacob winked at Phoebe who twisted the bottom of her sweater in her hands.

Eli slapped his hat against his thigh. "One dollar! Ain't no city boy going to outbid me."

The room grew silent as those attending the bid transferred their attention to the rivalry at the front of the room. Jacob motioned for a dollar fifty.

"Where you getting that kind of money, boy?"

Eli pulled out his pockets and counted his cash. "A dollar sixty-five is it. You're taking food out of my babies' mouths."

Jacob strolled to the front of the room. "A dollar seventy-five, and the cake is mine." He waited for Eli to say something, while hoping he wouldn't. Eli shoved his hat on his head and stormed out the door.

The smile on Phoebe's face was worth the money. Jacob lifted the cake and motioned his head toward a smaller table set up with two chairs. She nodded and followed.

"I got a little nervous for a minute," she said as Jacob pulled out her chair.

He laughed. "You and me both. But my plan worked like a charm." He sat across from her. "These types of things are the safest way for me to see you without Eli going berserk."

Phoebe cut two slices of the cake. "How's school?"

"Surprisingly good. Attendance stays regular, except for the Coffman kids and one or two others." He accepted the piece she gave him. "And we're off this week for Thanksgiving. I'm organizing a Christmas program. I'd like you to sing and play."

Her eyes widened. "I don't do that in public."

"Why not? You're good." Jacob stuck his fork of cake in his mouth and tasted heaven. "But not as good as this cake."

She laughed. The sound as musical and beautiful as a babbling brook. It's infectious sound made Jacob join in. The first time he heard her was over a piece of cake. He made a vow to hear her laugh more often.

Her cheeks flushed, and her eyes twinkled. Jacob couldn't remember seeing a more beautiful woman. His gaze flicked to where Viola held court with a dark-haired young man. The younger sister's attractiveness didn't hold a candle in his opinion. Her hazel eyes, though wide and innocent looking, couldn't compare to the intensity of Phoebe's. The rosebud mouth might be considered alluring if not kept in a perpetual pout. No, Phoebe was the woman he wanted to see when he went to sleep each evening and especially when he woke each morning.

The murmurs and chuckles of other couples filled the barn with a sense of gaiety. One side of the barn held tables for the men and their baker. On the other, families and married partners sat on bales of hay and ate their simple lunches.

Gone was the cloud of oppression hanging over Jacob's head from his travels across an impoverished country. The guilt over the death of a young woman showed signs of leaving.

Tucked away in a little known hollow in the Ozarks, life continued much the same as it had for centuries. Modern conveniences showed here and there, like the phone at Dixon's store, or the trucks running the back logging roads. If not for the moonshine issue, peace prevailed in the little town, and Jacob found himself wanting to be a permanent part of it. Wanderlust no longer had a grip on him.

"Jacob?"

"I'm sorry."

Phoebe crossed her arms. "Am I so boring you need to stare into space?"

"Not at all." He took the last bite of his dessert. "I've realized how much I like Pine Ridge, and want to stay." He placed a hand on her arm. "Especially with you by my side."

"I'd like that."

"So, you choose me?"

Her cheeks turned the prettiest pink he'd ever seen. "Yes."

"Let's tell Eli."

Her smile faded. "We can't. Not yet. Not until I've helped my father."

"But I can protect you as your fiancée."

"I've got to let Eli believe he still has a chance. He needs to trust me, Jacob. Then he will lead me to where the main still is."

"We found the still."

She shook her head. "That one isn't big enough. Not by a long shot. It couldn't possibly provide enough whiskey for flatbed trucks. That's an independent still. A lot of folks up here have them."

Jacob scratched his head. "I've never heard of something this large. Prohibition should have ended it."

"But it didn't." Phoebe covered the cake and rose. "Walk me out. I'm yours until we reach the wagon."

"Then let's walk real slow." He tucked her free arm in the crook of his elbow.

Her rising must have been the clue for the rest of the family because the kids stampeded outside. Grandma rose from her gaggle of friends, and Viola hooked her hand through the arm of the young man she'd eaten with.

Phoebe smiled into Jacob's face as he led her outside. They stopped and Jacob blinked against the brightness of the sun on a light layer of snow. Marring the pristine surface stood Eli with his shotgun aimed at Jacob's chest.

A shot rang out.

10

Jacob dove, taking Phoebe to the ground with him. Her breath whooshed past his cheek as she grunted. His side burned like someone stuck a hot match to it. The cake plate shattered, splattering them with frosting. A shard of glass drove itself into Jacob's hand.

He cupped Phoebe's face with his uninjured hand and stared into her eyes to make sure she was okay before he struggled to his feet. With a howl, he rushed Eli, striking the man with his shoulder and driving him into a tree. Two other men grabbed Jacob and pulled him off. He tried yanking free but the rush of adrenaline began to subside, letting him feel the pain of his wound.

"Are you crazy?!" The man's whiskey soaked breath washed over Jacob's face. "You shot me and could've killed somebody."

"The only person I want dead is you." Eli shoved against Jacob's chest. "If I hadn't had a drink, you'd be six feet under by tomorrow."

Jacob rose and hauled the man to his feet. "Go home, Eli. You're drunk." He yanked the shotgun out of his hands. "I'll return this when you get control of yourself."

He backed up, keeping an eye on the inebriated man until Eli cursed and stumbled down the road. Jacob lowered the shotgun and sagged against the tree.

"You're bleeding." Phoebe shoved aside his coat. "JJ send for the doctor." Her brother dashed away.

Jacob's knees trembled. "I'm fine. It's just a graze."

"You've got glass in your hand and blood soaking your clothes. You are not fine. I'm taking you home."

"Best words I've heard in a long time." He grinned.

"Stop funnin' me, Jacob. Get in the wagon."

"You're a bossy little thing, aren't you?" He tossed the shotgun in the back and climbed in beside the kids. Adrenaline wearing off, fatigue set in. He leaned against the side and closed his eyes.

"Don't die on me, Jacob." Phoebe yawed to the horses and slapped the reins.

"I wouldn't dream of it." Every jolt and bounce sent waves of agony through him. Despite the frigid temperature, perspiration beaded on his forehead. How in the world had he managed to take Eli to the ground?

Opening his eyes required strength he didn't have. Worry and rage over the possibility of Phoebe being killed had driven him past the pain. Even if the bullet had struck something vital, he'd have done the same thing. As long as he drew breath he'd save her with whatever strength God gave him.

"He's turning white." Noel poked him in the chest. "I think he's already dead."

"Did the bullet make a hole?" Grandma twisted around and peered at him.

Noel lifted Jacob's shirt. "Naw, just a groove, but it's bleeding something fierce."

"Darn. I've got a new silk handkerchief we could have pulled through a hole. Would've healed him right up. Nothing to do for a groove but stitch it and wait."

Jacob sucked in a breath. "I'm not dead. Just frozen." And he'd die before letting her pull anything through a hole of his. Before he knew it, he found himself pressed upon by every member of the Lillie family besides Grandma and Phoebe. The warmth of their bodies lulled him to sleep.

The wagon lurched to a halt. Jacob opened his eyes and allowed the children to help him from the wagon bed. Grandma shuffled through the door ahead of them.

"Viola, bring in your pa's cot." She reached above the mantel and grabbed a metal box. Inside sat a brown resin looking lump beside a pipe. "Shave off a bit of this and let him chew it. He'll feel good until the doctor gets here."

"What is it?" Jacob chewed his bottom lip.

"Gum opium. Take off your shirt. Noel, get me the kerosene."

Viola returned with the single-size bed and shoved it against the wall. Jacob collapsed on his back, his feet hanging off the end. Grandma cut a chunk of opium the size of a pea.

"I'm not letting you put that in my mouth." He bolted upright, glancing at Phoebe for help.

She smiled. "It *will* make you feel better, Jacob."

"I'm sure it will." He peeled off his shirt. With his prior addiction to alcohol, he didn't dare succumb to drugs no matter who gave them to him.

Grandma placed a hand on his shoulder, pushed him back onto the cot, took the bottle from Viola, then poured it over his wound. A thousand fire ants ate through him.

"Whoa." He jerked back to a sitting position. "Please, can we wait for the doctor? Or at least use whiskey to cleanse?"

"Whiskey costs more. I've healed more people in more years than you've lived, boy." Grandma poured more kerosene into the wound, renewing the burning. "But I ain't stitching you up. Don't worry."

Jacob hitched his breath then released it in a sigh. He'd been crazy to move to such a backwoods place. Didn't these people know opium was against the law? Much less shooting people. "Why aren't we calling the sheriff?"

"You ain't dead, boy." Grandma gathered up her supplies. "Eli didn't mean any harm. He's just smarting because Phoebe seems to enjoy your company more than his. He wouldn't have shot you if he'd been sober. No need to call the law. They got bigger fish to fry down in the city."

*

Phoebe laughed as Jacob argued with Grandma. She shook her head. Jacob acted like he'd never been doctored at home before. His grumbling reassured her he'd be all right, and she turned her attentions to planning dinner.

Before the blond-headed giant arrived on their doorstep, weeks would go by before the sound of joy escaped her lips. Now, it bubbled inside her and escaped like water from the soda springs.

Sitting down with him for a slice of cake at church had almost seemed like they were married. Facing him across a table every night wouldn't be a hardship. Not with his looks or his unthinking willingness to help anyone in need. Her grandmother pinned the man correctly on the night he'd arrived. An angel sent straight from heaven to help the Lillie family.

JJ burst through the door followed by Doctor Fox, a big burly man with a face red from a love of whiskey. Dr. Fox headed straight to the cot.

Jacob leaned on one elbow. "Thank the Lord. Grandma Lillie poured kerosene in me and tried to get me to chew a chunk of opium."

The doctor's bushy eyebrows rose. "Kerosene won't hurt, and when I start stitching, you'll most likely wish you'd chewed the opium. I've nothing to numb you with but that or whiskey."

"I beg to differ on the kerosene, Doc. It hurt quite a bit. As for the whiskey and opium, I'd rather grit my teeth and bear it."

"Suit yourself." The doctor opened his black bag and bent over Jacob.

Phoebe stepped to his side in case the man needed help. "Hold my hand, Jacob."

He slipped his hand in hers. "I feel better already."

"Always the flirt, Mr. Wright."

"Honest." He clinched his jaw with the first thrust of the needle and squeezed Phoebe's hand tight enough to grind her bones together. Together, they hissed like a couple of spitting cats.

When the doctor finished, he handed Jacob a bottle of pills. "For infection. Stay in bed for a few days, and you'll be able to run around again after Thanksgiving." He winked. "Next time someone shoots you, don't tackle them to the ground. You did more damage than good."

Jacob laughed. "I'll try to remember that."

Phoebe patted his shoulder. "Get some sleep. I'll wake you when supper's done."

She wrapped a shawl around her shoulders and stepped outside. With the sun setting, the temperature dropped. Her breath plumed out from her mouth like dragon's fire.

Phoebe leaned against the side of the smoke shed and stared into the night sky. Could she pluck a star from the sky? If she could, she'd give it to Jacob, declare her love for him, and tell Eli Coffman to jump in the lake.

She hadn't been afraid when the shot rang out. Gunfire was something you heard a lot on the mountain. But when she'd seen the blood spreading through Jacob's coat, her heart had stopped. It didn't matter that he'd fought Eli afterward. She'd seen herself how a bear can keep running after taking a bullet. It's when the body stops long enough for the mind to register the damage that matters. Some men have been shot, continued the fight, and then dropped dead once the pain registered.

Remembering Jacob's shocked expression when Grandma started caring for him, Phoebe smiled. City folk. Most of the homegrown mountain remedies worked just fine.

She loved the fact he'd be around for a few

days. Grandma wouldn't let him go back to his house no matter how much he whined. The woman loved having someone to care for. The Lillie children didn't count much anymore. All but Maggie could take care of themselves, unless sick or hurt.

"Phoebe."

She jerked. "Pa? You've got to stop sneaking up and scaring me like that."

He stepped from around the corner of the shed. "I heard someone got shot."

"Just a graze. Jacob Wright, the new teacher, won my cake in a bid against Eli. Eli didn't take the news well." Phoebe laughed.

"You could've been killed."

"He was drunk. He didn't mean anything."

Her pa ran his hands through his hair. "It's the Devil's brew, Phoebe. That's why I've got to put a stop to it. It's tearing this hollow apart."

She placed a hand on his arm. "Why you, Pa?"

"Because the men trust me. I'm one of them. An outsider wouldn't get close."

"How involved is Eli?"

"Right smack in the middle." He brushed a loose strand of hair away from her face. "There's something I want you to do. Tomorrow morning, go to Dixon's store. Tell that old coot about the teacher being shot. Tell him we're out of the whiskey we use for medicine and ask if you can buy a pint. I'll check with you in the evening to see whether you were successful."

"Dixon doesn't sell that at his store."

"I'm not sure if he does or not. If he says no, ask for the cough syrup in the red jar. That's the stuff." Her pa kissed her cheek and dashed back into the woods.

Phoebe shook her head and unlatched the shed door. She hacked off a chunk of ham, locked things up tight, then headed back to the house. It didn't make sense. Wouldn't her pa know whether Dixon sold the stuff or not? Was he trying to trick the man?

She decided that was it. He wanted to know who was doing the right thing in Pine Ridge through the process of elimination. Her steps quickened. Finally, something constructive she could do to help.

Jacob's snores greeted her when she stepped into the warmth of the cabin. The children played quietly in front of the fire, while Grandma darned socks.

Phoebe dropped the ham in a pan of simmering beans and went to check on Jacob. She laid the back of her hand across his forehead. Cool.

"Stop drooling over the man." Viola tossed a ball of yarn she'd rolled into the basket at her feet. "Just because he knocked you down, doesn't mean he cares for you. Jacob is the type of man that would take a bullet for anyone."

"And I suppose you wish he would've taken one for you." Phoebe put her fists on her hips. "Men swarm around you like bees to honey. Why do you think you have to have Jacob too?" She blinked against the tears stinging her eyes and knelt beside the cot.

Jacob's eyes fluttered open and he laid a hand over hers. "Viola doesn't stand a chance, Phoebe. You've already stolen my heart." With a deep breath, he went back to sleep.

He'd spoken the words so softly Phoebe thought maybe he hadn't said them at all. Maybe they'd been a dream she wanted so badly, she imagined them. A quick glance at Viola's cherry-red face soothed her fear. She smiled and laid her cheek against his hand.

11

Where are you going?"

Phoebe paused with one hand on the door and turned toward Jacob. "To Dixon's store."

"Wait. I'll go with you." He swung his legs over the side of the bed.

"You're supposed to rest. I'll be back in an hour."

"I don't want you out alone with Eli running loose."

"If anything, Eli will apologize. He doesn't pose a threat to me." Phoebe squared her shoulders and stepped outside. If she stayed any longer, Jacob would know she lied. People always told her that whatever she felt showed on her face. She was nothing more than an open book.

Icy branches cracked over head as Phoebe set off down the road. Despite the cold, she chose to walk. It gave her the chance to think.

When she'd vowed to help her father, she hadn't

known she'd be an errand girl. The monotony of her life left her craving the action she read about in books. She could shoot as well as her brother. With her fixed shoe, she could move as quickly as the next person. And her brain worked faster than most around the hollow.

A cardinal flew overhead, its scarlet plumage startling against the tree's bare branches. Despite the harshness of life in the hollow, beauty still resounded. Phoebe needed to remind herself every day. Life got better. Jacob's arrival proved that. At least it provided light in her dreary life.

By the time she arrived at the store, the brisk air had invigorated her. She smiled at the two men just inside the door. With the cold weather, whittling was set aside and they hunched over a checker board in front of a wood burning stove. They nodded in acknowledgement and turned back to their game.

"Phoebe." Dixon clapped his hands together. "What can I get for you?"

She sidled up to the counter and in a low voice, said, "We're out of our medicinal whiskey. The teacher was shot yesterday."

"I heard that sad news, but we don't sell whiskey here."

"What about the stuff in the red jars?" She winked.

"You got something in your eye, sweetie?"

Dixon scratched his chin. "I've got baking soda in red cans, but that's it. Are you sure you're thinking about the right stuff? Don't you know where your pa buys his moonshine?"

Phoebe straightened and shook her head. "I was hoping you did."

"Sorry. If I was to sell it here, the Feds would shut me down." He leaned across the counter. "Knock on any neighbor's door. My bet is nine out of ten of them have some or can tell you where to get it. Hope Mr. Wright is up and about soon. It won't do to have our teacher down."

"It's just a flesh wound. He'll be fine." Phoebe captured her bottom lip between her teeth. She pulled her jacket tighter around her and moved outside.

One of the men followed. "Miss Lillie."

"Mr. Owens." She turned to face the husky man in faded overalls and patched flannel hunting jacket.

"I've got some in my wagon over there. A dollar ninety-five a pint." His bloodshot eyes narrowed. "But you didn't get it from me."

Phoebe swallowed hard and slipped two dollars from her pocket. "I swear." Did Pa actually want her to buy some if Dixon couldn't provide? She handed over the money. The man would be suspicious if she changed her mind now. Not to mention, he gave her the creeps. His eyes traveled over her with the speed of a snail. She shuddered and wished for a hot bath.

He sneered and pocketed the cash then handed her a mason jar of clear liquid. "You won't find better anywhere in these parts." Mr. Owens spun on his heel and headed into the store.

Wonderful. Phoebe glanced around and hoped no one would see her clutching an armful of illegal brew. She opened her coat, stuffed the jar inside, and zipped up around it. All the way home, its sloshing reminded her of what she carried. She'd never had the unpleasant task before. There always seemed to be a jar in the pantry. She'd never questioned how it got there.

Phoebe halted in her front yard and watched as Noel pushed Peter in a tree swing. She needed to leave Pa a note, but sneaking to the back of the house and into the woods would alert the younger boys' curiosity. They'd be sure to follow. She sighed and pushed open the front door.

"Where you been?" Grandma waved a wooden spoon in her direction. "I don't mind getting breakfast for the family, but a little warning would be nice. Instead, I'm shook awake by children whining."

"I'm sorry. I took a walk." Phoebe climbed the loft to her bed, avoiding Jacob's gaze.

"A walk? Must be nice to have a life of leisure. Taking a nice stroll before chores. Today's wash day too. You know it's going to take a while since the sun's hiding behind them clouds." Grandma's grumbling followed her as she shoved the pint beneath her cot and tossed a dirty dress on top of it. Having a family her size didn't allow for privacy. She'd have to find a way to get out of the house after dark.

She rushed to her grandmother's side and washed the dishes from breakfast. Prior experiences from childhood told her she'd have to skip the morning meal. If you aren't there to eat on time, you don't eat. In Grandma's word, the Lillie household wasn't a fancy mansion with servants to wait on a person hand and foot.

Jacob shifted on his cot. Phoebe tossed aside her rag and rushed over to place a hand on his forehead. Cool. She smiled. The city man had more spunk then she'd thought. She brushed a curl away from his face. Had he really said she possessed his heart? Could a man this beautiful love a girl from the hills?

*

Jacob remained still and enjoyed the feel of Phoebe's hand on his skin. Soft as a feather and as soothing as a summer rain. He fought to keep a smile from his lips. If she knew he faked sleeping, she'd raise the roof. Someday, her Irish temper would get her in trouble. Hopefully, he'd be able to save the day, riding in on a chocolate-covered mule like a tarnished knight.

A great sense of emptiness fell on him when she

rose and moved away. Fool. He should've opened his eyes. Then she would've stayed and talked. No, he needed to allow her to finish her work. Then maybe she'd keep him company.

He peeked through his lashes. She stood at the sink drying plates as Grandma washed. His gaze traveled from her shapely calves to slender waist to thick hair. What a feast for the eyes God made when he crafted Phoebe Lillie. Jacob sighed.

She turned and wrapped the dish towel around her neck before hurrying to his side. "Are you in pain, Jacob?"

"No." He grinned. "Just enjoying the view."

"Stop." She whipped the towel from around her neck and popped him in the leg. "You're embarrassing me."

"And you're injuring a wounded man." He reached for her hand and pulled her to sit beside him. "What's your response to my statement last night?"

Her eyes widened. "What do you mean?" Her gaze flicked to where Grandma disappeared out the back door.

"About you stealing my heart."

Her face reddened. "It made me feel good."

"But?"

"There's the problem of Eli." She twisted the hem of her apron with her free hand. "And Viola."

"Not really. We're both openly courting you,

and Viola needs to pester some other guy. I want to move past the dating phase and right into a serious relationship. But as far as anyone else is concerned, you haven't decided between me and Eli." Did he move too fast? Although Phoebe seemed to have the strength of iron, she was as skittish as a rabbit. Her self-esteem was lower than a frog's belly.

Her eyes glittered with unshed tears. "You want a relationship with me?"

Jacob squeezed her hand. "Not like that. I want to marry you, Phoebe Lillie. I want to shout it from the mountaintop. I know you're helping your father right now and Eli plays into that. I'll wait."

Her breath shuddered. "There's nothing I'd like more than to be your wife. It is soon, Jacob. What if you don't want to stay in the hollow? This is my home. I can't imagine living anywhere else."

He leaned back against the pillows. The lure of a home outweighed the wanderlust he'd held on to for the last five years. A wife and children beckoned him to stay. Then another woman's face reared to the forefront of his mind. A blond porcelain-skinned stranger.

He'd been responsible for her death as sure as if he'd pulled the trigger that stopped her heart. He hadn't jumped in front of a bullet that time. Whiskey had dulled his reflexes, and the city streetwalker fell in a pool of her own blood, all because of the five dollars in Jacob's pocket. She'd been the first to die because of his gun.

His gaze locked on Phoebe's and he nodded. Despite silly superstitions and the rampant lure of home brewed whiskey, with God's help, he could stay in this backwoods hollow and make a good life for them and any children God decided to send.

Phoebe smiled and laid his hand back in his lap. "Then I accept your proposal, Jacob Wright. But we keep it secret for now. Even from my family. Viola has loose lips and will feel rejected by you. The news would be all over by daylight tomorrow."

"Our secret it is."

The blush returned to her cheeks and she rose. "I've got chores to do."

"First, tell me why you headed to Dixon's store so early this morning."

She glanced around the room then bent to whisper in his ear. "I had an errand to run for Pa. I'll tell you later. When no one's around."

"I hope so, Phoebe. I don't want any more secrets between us."

"I promise." With a swish of her skirt, she headed back to the dishes.

Jacob sat and let his legs hang over the cot. A bullet graze shouldn't be enough to keep a man down. There had to be something he could do around the place to help. Besides, he couldn't keep an eye on his beautiful Irish hillbilly by lying around in bed. The thought of her wandering the countryside trying to put a stop to moonshiners sent a chill down his spine. They hadn't killed anyone yet, and he didn't want her to be the first.

"What are you doing out of bed?" Phoebe planted fists on her slender hips.

"I'm going to do something around here to earn my keep. I can at least help the little ones with their chores." Jacob stood and balanced with one hand on a nearby chair. With a deep breath, he took a step then another. "See. Almost as good as new."

Phoebe rolled her eyes. "Foolish man. Don't let me stop you from doing something idiotic."

Jacob laughed. "Okay, I won't." He shuffled to the front door and swung it open. His smile faded.

Eli Coffman frowned from the top step.

12

Y ou're staying here?" Eli's face turned the color of a ripe tomato. "I didn't hurt you that bad."

"Just for now, Eli." Jacob stepped onto the porch. "At the Lillies' request. The doctor said to take it easy because of the stitches."

"Pshaw. Stitches ain't nothing. You're being a pansy. Ain't fittin' or fair that you stay here. How am I supposed to win Phoebe's heart with you staying under the same roof? Plus, it don't look right."

Jacob laughed and leaned against the railing. "I think there are more than enough chaperones. What do you really want, Eli?"

"I came to apologize. In my drunkenness, I could've hit Phoebe instead of you."

"Well, go ahead." Jacob inclined his head toward the door. "Knock. She's home." He left Eli's mouth hanging open and sauntered to where the horses grazed behind a split-rail fence. The nearby barn sported a door hanging from one hinge. Something Jacob could do.

He headed to a shed and retrieved the necessary tools. Within minutes, the door swung freely and without a squeak. The stitches in his side wouldn't allow him to do lifting of any kind, but he could feed the chickens that clacked nearby.

"Hey, Peter, I'll do that." Jacob took the bucket from the boy and began scattering the feed.

"Okay. Are you doing all my chores today?" Peter climbed the fence and straddled a post. "'Cause my next one is sweeping out the hen house. I hate that job. It smells something awful. Then Noah and me have to clean out the hog pen. Why is that, Jacob? They're just going to get it all dirty again."

Jacob laughed. "I'm not sure my side is up to sweeping or mucking out a pig pen. I'd best do this and see what else I can help with that's relatively easy."

The boy stared at the ground. "Are you going to marry Phoebe? Because if my pa don't come home, we need a man of the house. JJ thinks he's it, but he's still a kid, despite his big head. I miss Pa."

"He'll be back, Peter. Trust God. If something had happened to your pa, you'd have heard." He laid a hand on the boy's shoulder.

It wasn't right that Ben Lillie kept his children and mother worrying. Jacob fought back the temptation to tell Peter his pa only kept away out of a misguided notion of keeping his family out of harm's way. If the man followed the Lord, he should place his trust there, and care for his family.

Loud voices carried from the house. Jacob shoved the bucket back at Peter. Holding his hand firmly against his side, he dashed to the house, and barged through the door.

Phoebe yanked her arm free of Eli's grip. "How dare you question my virtue."

"I have every right as your future husband." Eli's face contorted. "Only a harlot lets a man she isn't married to sleep under the same roof."

"I never said I'd marry you." Phoebe backed against the counter. When she grasped the handle of an iron skillet and raised it above her head, Jacob rushed in.

"Whoa." He took the pan from her hand then turned to Eli. "I told you, nothing is going on here. I'll move back to my place tonight if that will set your mind at ease."

"But—" Phoebe stepped forward.

"No." Jacob set her weapon of choice on the counter. "I won't be party to ruining your reputation."

Eli lifted his chin. "Good. Now we're back on fair ground." The man spun and stormed from the house.

The man was insane. Did he honestly believe

his heavy-handed ways would win Phoebe's heart? Jacob shook his head then grinned at Phoebe. "As much as I would've loved seeing you bash his head with a skillet, what were you thinking?"

She shrugged. "He grabbed me."

Jacob lifted her hair. "Are you sure you aren't a redhead under there?"

"Stop." She slapped his hand away but not before he saw her smile.

Jacob moved to the cot and sat down. He'd be fine at home. The bad thing was he couldn't keep an eye on Phoebe. During his travels, he'd come to recognize human nature. Eli Coffman carried a short fuse. It was only a matter of time before he blew. Jacob didn't want Phoebe caught in the blast. As soon as he could move without his stitches pulling, he'd scour the mountain for Ben Lillie and convince him to come home.

*

Phoebe handed Jacob his jacket. "Not too strenuous. If you start bleeding, or the wound gets inflamed, call the doctor."

Jacob cupped her face. "Yes, mother."

She turned her lips to his palm. "I'm serious. People die from infection."

"I'll be fine."

Phoebe watched him leave. Her heart dropped. She should be going with him, setting up house in the little cabin. Instead, she stayed here to carry on a pretense with a man she despised. *It'd better be worth it, Pa.*

She hadn't told Jacob Eli would be picking her up after supper for a stroll in the moonlight. He'd be livid if he found out. Beneath his angelic appearance lurked...something, held in check. She felt it. Jacob carried a burden she wanted to ease, a strength she wanted to rely on, and a sense of right and wrong she appreciated. But over all that, he seemed capable of great rage if pushed far enough. She'd seen it in the way his eyes hardened when he looked at Eli.

"You should be ashamed of yourself." Viola climbed from the loft. "Throwing yourself at two men. I saw you make plans with Eli, then kiss Jacob's hand. And people think I'm the one with loose morals."

"How long have you been up there?"

"Long enough to know you're up to something." Viola crossed her arms. "So, what is it? It can't be that you're undecided. There's no comparison between Jacob and Eli. One is clearly a better choice."

"Why do you care?" Phoebe removed her apron and hung it on a hook. "You've been seen with that dark-haired Wood boy. John, right? He's more your age. Stick him with him."

"I'm a woman now. I want a man."

She wanted Jacob, Phoebe knew. Well, she

couldn't have him. For once, a man preferred Phoebe, and she wouldn't give him up without a fight. Not even to her sister. When he looked at her, her blood coursed with a fiery intensity. When he touched her, she almost forgot the reasons she'd vowed to stay pure until marriage. Phoebe shook her head. No, Jacob Wright was a treasure worth fighting over.

Viola plopped in front of the radio and studied her nails. "I wonder what Eli would say about you kissing Jacob? He might find that bit of news interesting."

"Why would you do something like that?" Phoebe's heart threatened to burst through her ribcage. "I've done nothing to hurt you. You've got beauty, brains, and any beau you want. Why are you so set on taking mine?"

"I find the men in the hollow simple. Boring." Viola flipped her hair. "Jacob comes from a different world. He's exciting and handsome. He could take me away from here."

Phoebe squared her shoulders. "He doesn't want you."

Viola's eyes turned to ice. "Well, if I can't have him, neither can you." She rose and stomped out of the house.

Phoebe fell into the nearest chair. Why did her sister hate her so? *God, please let Jacob be made of sterner stuff than Viola could penetrate.* Phoebe would wither and die without him as sure as the leaves dried up in winter.

A banging on the front door pulled her from her musings. With a sigh, she grabbed her pa's flannel jacket and tossed it around her shoulders. A stroll during the winter. What was Eli thinking? She opened the door and stepped outside.

Viola flashed her a grin and sashayed around the corner of the house. Phoebe frowned then forced a smile to her lips and greeted Eli.

"Ready for our walk?" He tucked his tongue into his cheek and marched off. Phoebe shrugged and followed, almost running to keep up with his furious pace. "Where's the fire?"

"Don't feel much like talking." Eli shoved his hands in his pockets.

"Okay. We don't have to." Phoebe cast a sideways glance at him. His jaw twitched from the pressure he exerted. Something had him riled. She searched her mind for a way of calming him.

"I'm real sorry you didn't win the cake bid." Phoebe tried to sound flirtatious, but the words came out a whisper.

"Sure you are." Eli hunched his shoulders then led her off the road and onto a little-traveled path.

"Where are we going?"

"Somewhere we can be alone."

Phoebe's steps faltered. Being alone in the woods with Eli could not be good. "I can't be gone long. I've got chores to do."

"Won't take long."

She shivered from more than the cold. They reached a small clearing, and Eli turned to face her. His face resembled the rough bark of an oak. Phoebe shrank back from the heat of his stare.

"Seems you've been kissing the teacher." Eli shook his head. "You ain't the woman I thought you were. Now, don't get me wrong, Phoebe. I still want you for my wife, but you need to be taught a lesson."

"Excuse me?" Viola did it. She betrayed her. Phoebe could hardly believe it.

"It's got to be me or the teacher." Eli sneered. "And it'll be me, 'cause the teacher won't be around if you choose him."

"I'm just using him, Eli. It doesn't mean anything. I'm trying to find my pa. Jacob is helping."

He leaned close, his tongue leaving a wet trail up her neck and over her jawline. "That's real good. Your pa using you like a stool pigeon. You're pa is fine. I see him every day, working the still, running the whiskey. You name it. We've a big order to fill. Now, you don't look surprised to hear the news. Why is that? Could be Ben is using you to ferret out the traitors."

Phoebe shook her head, swallowing bile, and backed up until a tree stopped her retreat. "I've been helping Pa. That's why I know. He sends me on simple errands to fetch stuff and send messages. I swear." She turned her head and closed her eyes.

"That's good. Soon, you can help first hand." Eli pressed against her.

Tears squeezed from her eyes. Her bosom heaved.

Eli laughed. "Got you all excited now, don't I? Well, what would that pretty teacher think if I was to defile you? Would he still want you? 'Cause I would."

She shoved against him. He stumbled back, giving her a moment to flee. She slapped aside branches as she ran. His footsteps thundered behind her.

Eli grasped her hair and pulled her to an abrupt stop. She shrieked as he spun her around then pummeled his chest. His lips peeled back from tobacco stained teeth.

The first punch knocked her to the ground. The second made her world grow dark as he lifted her dress.

13

J acob lit the lamp in the center of his table and leaned his head on folded arms. He'd proposed to Phoebe. Not the romantic gesture he'd always envisioned, but he'd done it nevertheless. He'd chosen to leave behind the wildness of his past and promised to love one woman for the rest of his days.

When Phoebe had laid her soft lips against his palm, he'd wanted nothing more than to pull her into his arms and kiss her until she swooned. Melt her prim and proper exterior. But the thought of being brained with an iron skillet held him back.

He straightened and smiled. God's blessings continued to shower upon him. Finally, his past deeds were laid to rest. A bright future beckoned.

The front door shook as someone banged on it. Jacob lurched to his feet and yanked it open. JJ bent over panting for breath.

"What is it?" Jacob's grip on the door handle turned his knuckles white. The look on the boy's face stabbed him.

"You've got to come. Phoebe went for a walk with Eli and hasn't come home. I ran by his place before coming here. He was sitting down at the dinner table. Said he left her hours ago." JJ raised a tear-stained face to Jacob's. "Something's happened to her."

"I'll get my gun." Jacob grabbed his pistol from the mantel and hurriedly shrugged into his jacket. Why did she insist on investigating alone? Her disappearance had to have something to do with the moonshine. "Did Eli say where they went for a walk?"

"He said up around the courting tree, but I've been there. No sign of her." JJ grabbed Jacob's arm. "I'm a good tracker, Mr. Wright. If they'd been there, I would've seen signs."

Fear gripped Jacob's heart with a marble fist. Phoebe knew these woods. She wouldn't be lost. He agreed with JJ. Something had happened to her. Lord, *don't let us be too late*. "Grab the lantern. We'll check the trails opposite the tree."

"I did."

"Then we'll head farther up the road. She can't have vanished." The boy's face fell with Jacob's sharp words. "I'm sorry."

JJ nodded. "I know. I'm scared too. Viola's done nothing but cry since she heard. Said it's all her fault, but I can't make any sense of her words."

What had the fool girl done now? Jacob closed the door behind them and took the lantern from JJ. Together they set off at a jog. Pain throbbed through his side with each jar of his foot striking the road. Jacob grit his teeth. He'd worry about his injury later.

God, please. He didn't know what to pray other than those two words. If he prayed for her to be safe and found her injured or worse, what would that do to his faith? His spirit yearned for the surety of a possible answer. Life had taught him you didn't always get what you prayed for and sometimes, what you prayed for wasn't really what you wanted. In this case, he wanted Phoebe to be alive. Something he wanted more than anything he'd ever asked for.

The burning in his side made keeping up with the jogging JJ difficult. The pain subsided some by holding his arm firm against himself but that kept the gun sticking out at an unnatural angle. JJ halted fast enough for Jacob to collide with him. The barrel of his pistol jabbed the boy in the back.

JJ spared him a cool glance, then dashed to their right. Inside the tree line, he slowed, his gaze sweeping the ground around them.

"What, exactly, are you hoping to see?" Jacob leaned against a tree to catch his breath.

"Phoebe would've stayed close to the road for a walk with Eli. He might have been able to lure her a few feet away, but no more than that. Plus, she wouldn't have wanted to be gone long. Despite her acting like she liked him. I know better." JJ scooted some leaves with his foot. "My guess is, they weren't walking more than twenty minutes. Thirty at the most. If I'm figuring right, they would've stopped somewhere along here or on the other side. Shine that lantern a little closer, okay?"

"You'll make a good lawman someday, James." Jacob stepped up and lifted his free arm. With the glow from the lantern, he could discern where the ground showed signs of a struggle. Packed dirt swept free of leaves. Bushes sported broken branches. He whipped around. "Phoebe!" Her name echoed through the night's frosty air.

He moved in a zig-zag pattern across the road and back, then across again, holding the lantern above his head. This wasn't like her to be gone past dark. Too many responsibilities waited for her at home. Even he knew that. His heart pained with each beat, hammering hard enough he feared it'd bust out of his chest. When he'd begun to lose hope, he spotted a foot sticking from beneath a juniper bush.

"JJ, over here." Jacob set the lantern on the ground and shoved aside the branches. Needles poked his hands as he dug her out. "Oh, sweetheart." He fell to his knees at her side and scooped her into his arms.

JJ grabbed the lantern and followed as Jacob rose then sprinted down the road toward the house. Jacob cradled Phoebe's swollen and bleeding face against his chest and drove away all stabs of pain from his side. Her moans as he ran signaled to him she still breathed. God had answered his prayer. Again, not as he'd expected but at least the big guy still listened to a sinner such as he.

When the house came into view, JJ dashed ahead and flung open the door. Jacob followed and, with as much care as possible, laid Phoebe on the cot he'd occupied recently. He stared at her battered face.

Her bottom lip had been split. Blood dried in the corner. One eye was swollen twice its size, and he doubted she'd be able to open it when she woke. A bruised lump rose on her cheek. Her sweater hung in tatters. His gaze traveled over the rest of her as he examined the torn and stained dress.

He'd kill the man with his bare hands.

"He didn't take her, did he?" Tears spilled from JJ's eyes.

Jacob shook his head. His voice trembled. "I don't know." He didn't see any reason to tell the boy what he believed to be the truth. "Run for the doctor, would you?"

He darted out the door before Jacob lifted his head. "Grandma, could you fetch a rag and cool water?"

"Already done." The woman handed him a pan. "You wash her face. I'll take care of her arms and legs. That beast took what only a husband should have, didn't he?"

Jacob nodded, and brushed the tears from his face. "Where's Viola?"

Her gaze pierced his. "She ain't come home since JJ left to look for his sister."

Jacob shrugged. He'd find out what she meant about things being her fault when she returned.

Phoebe groaned when he touched the scrap of soaked cotton to her swollen eye. She reached up and tried to push him away.

Jacob captured her hand in his. "Don't, honey. You've been hurt."

"Eli." Her words sounded hoarse.

"Don't talk now. We'll ask you questions later." When the sight of her bruised body no longer caused him to clinch his fists with a need to punch someone, and the desire to kill left him. Then, he might be in the right frame of mind to talk.

She gave a barely perceptible shake of her head. "Eli got angry because I kissed you."

"How would he know about that?"

"I told him." Viola's sobs shook her shoulders. "I got mad and thought telling him would be a good way to get back at Phoebe." She turned her red-rimmed eyes to Jacob. "I never thought he'd do this. Honest. He told me he loves her."

Jacob gritted his teeth hard enough to send a sharp pain through his temple. The girl's stupid jealousy could've gotten Phoebe killed.

"Get out of my sight." He spit the words between tight lips. "We'll talk more about this later. Make yourself useful and go take care of the little ones."

She choked back another cry and whirled to do his bidding. Her younger siblings sat the kitchen table, tears streaming silently down their cheeks. Jacob gave Viola another glare before turning back to Phoebe.

"I'll kill him. I swear I will." He continued swabbing her face.

"Get in line, young man." The door slammed shut. "I'm Ben Lillie, and this is my house. I'll see that justice is done. Who did this to my girl?"

Jacob jumped to his feet. "Eli Coffman, sir." The man stood close to six feet, only an inch above Jacob's height. His brown beard held bits of dry leaves. A strong odor of yeast emanated from him. Sticking out of the bib of the man's overalls was the handle of a sawed-off shotgun, a hog's leg, the mountain people called the gun.

"Where's JJ?"

"I sent him for the doctor."

Ben nodded then knelt beside his daughter. "Phoebe, I'm here. I'll take care of this for you."

"No, Pa." She tried to rise to one elbow and fell

back.

Jacob squeezed past her father, ignoring the man's stern look. "Stay still."

"I can't help if you kill him."

"What are you talking about?" Ben took off his floppy hat and slapped it against his leg.

"Putting away the moonshiners." She peered at him through one eye. "I have to continue to play along so you can find out who's behind it. So we can clean up the hollow."

"Look what he's done to you. He took something precious from you." Ben pulled a deep breath through his nose. "The man's crazy to lift a hand against you. If you don't want me to kill him, then I'll make sure he wishes he was dead." He pushed to his feet. "I'll have him looking every bit as colorful as you do."

"I'd like to go too, Mr. Lillie." Jacob squared his shoulders and stuck out a hand. "Jacob Wright, at your service."

"Didn't the pip squeak already shoot you once?"

"Just a graze."

Ben nodded. "You the one my girl loves?"

"I hope so." Jacob cast a glance at Phoebe.

"All right. You can hold me back from actually killing the man. Make sure I don't do something that will land me in jail. Viola, you come on. Someone will need to watch his children while I pound on him."

With one more glance at Phoebe, Jacob followed her father out the door. They walked in silence, the only sound was the fall of their footsteps on the road. A muscle twitched in Ben's jaw. Jacob fought back the urge to ask the man where'd he'd been for the last few weeks and how he found out about Phoebe's beating.

A mixed-breed dog bayed at their approach, and Eli stepped onto his porch, cradling a shotgun. "Down from the mountain, Ben?"

"Got me some business to tend to." With slow movements, Ben pulled the hog's leg from his bib. Jacob shot out a hand to stop him. Ben shrugged him off and propped the gun against a tree. "Viola, scoot into the house."

Eli stepped aside and allowed her access before dropping his weapon.

"What possessed you to lay a hand on my Phoebe?" Ben crossed his arms.

Eli shrugged. "She's my intended and kissed another man. Now, ain't no other man that will want her."

Jacob stepped forward. "I want her."

This time, Ben stopped him. "I ain't heard no words of y'all marrying. You haven't asked my blessing."

"Didn't see no need. She's a grown woman." Eli leaned against a post. "Before I take her as my wife, she needs to learn her place."

"So you left her, injured and unconscious, lying in the cold beneath a bush?" Jacob clinched his fists. If Ben didn't charge soon, he'd lose his chance to Jacob.

"Can't show weakness."

Ben charged with a roar. The impact of his body drove Eli into the porch railing with a crack as sharp as gunfire. The sound of pummeling fists drowned out anything else. Viola's pale face shone from the window.

Jacob hovered over the men thrashing on the ground. It took every ounce of willpower he possessed not to join in the melee. It was clear, Ben would emerge the victor, but Eli's wiry strength kept the fight going longer than Jacob had anticipated. When Eli bent over and spit out a tooth, Jacob intervened and dragged Ben off him.

"He's had enough."

Ben wiped a bloody lip on his sleeve. "You touch my daughter in any way that isn't cherishing again, and I'll kill you." He grinned. "But I doubt she'll let you get close to her now. Mayhap she puts a bullet in you herself. Come on, Viola." He grabbed his hat from where it had fallen and headed up the road.

Eli laughed. "Don't forget who you work for, Benjamin Lillie."

14

Phoebe brushed her fingertips over the bruises on her face. Her right eye was still swollen, although it had opened a slit. Her lip hurt when she talked or laughed, so for several days, she'd done neither. The only good thing to come out of Eli's rape was that Pa tended to stay close to home.

Tears threatened. Phoebe sniffed. She also avoided Jacob, and that hurt more than the cuts and marks from Eli's attempt to lay claim to her. The man might have taken her body, he might have temporarily taken her spirit, but he would never take her heart. Although her love for Jacob hadn't dimmed a bit, she knew he couldn't want her now. Not out of anything but pity.

"I'm so sorry." Viola stared up at her from the bed. "I had no idea this would happen."

Phoebe drew breath sharply through her nose. "This is what jealousy does." She turned so her sister could get a good long look. "I'm trying not to let my heart harden toward you, but right now, I can't bear to lay eyes on you. You who have it all.

"Men follow after you like dogs after a bitch in heat. Yet you couldn't let me have this one thing. All I've done is work for this family. Care for you young'uns. This is the reward I get." She grabbed her shawl from the hook, not caring when it caught and ripped. The sound was like the sound of her heart breaking. "I hope you're happy."

She closed her ears to the sound of her sister's sobs. It had taken all her strength to lie in bed while the traitor lay next to her. Well, no more. She would take up Pa's rifle and keep working at clearing the mountain of illegal moonshine. At least of the magnitude that was going on right then.

She'd grown up with whiskey on the gums of a teething baby or poured open a wound to disinfect, but what was happening on the mountain was way past anything they'd had happen before. Someone would end up dead before it came to an end, and she'd do everything in her power to make sure it wasn't one of her family members.

Without acknowledging Grandma or Pa, Phoebe took the rifle from the mantel and stormed out the front door. Feet pounded behind her.

"Where you going, girl?" Pa stopped on the top step of the porch.

"To get me a coon, where do you think?" She whirled and glared.

"I took care of him. He won't be bothering you. You can't go shoot a man in cold blood, sweetheart." Pa walked slowly toward her, his gaze on hers, one hand stretched to take the rifle. "I would have killed him myself if not for the teacher."

Phoebe sagged to the ground and let her sobs overtake her. "He won't want me now."

Pa knelt beside her and pulled her into his arms like he used to do when she was a child. "He says he does. Told Eli he did. Now, he don't seem like a liar to me." Pa rocked back and forth. "You're the same sweet Phoebe you was yesterday."

"I'm not." She rubbed her face against his coat, breathing in the familiar scents of tobacco and wood smoke. "I'm harder and broken, all at the same time."

"God can heal you."

"God has forgotten about me."

Pa pulled her to her feet. "Come on into the house, daughter. Let's get some food in your belly and then you put your feet up and work on that purty quilt by the fire. We'll all take care of anything else. You deserve a rest."

"I missed you, Pa." She slipped her arms around his waist.

"I ain't going anywhere."

She hoped not. A girl had her limits, and at the age of nineteen, Phoebe had reached hers.

*

Jacob rode his mule past the Lillie place. Everything in him wanted to stop and check on Phoebe, but Ben had sent word to let her have some time. Half a mile down the road, he spotted Viola duck into the woods, a cardboard suitcase in her hand.

Not wanting the girl to race away before he could see what she was up to, Jacob slid from the mule's back and tied the reins to a tree. He followed in the direction Viola had gone until she appeared again in a small clearing. She ran into the waiting arms of John Wood.

What was the girl up to now? He ducked behind a juniper bush.

"Where are we going?" Viola handed her case to John.

"We'll get hitched in Compton, then come back to live with my folks, what did you think?" John shook his head. "I ain't got no money. All I have is the family dirt, unless you want me making moonshine."

"No." She glanced over her shoulder. "I just want to get married and get away from my family. They hate me, John. My sister can't stand the sight of me. If they knew I was carrying your baby, well …"

So, the little minx had gotten herself in trouble. No wonder she was in such a hurry to snag a husband. Since she couldn't get Jacob, she'd settle on the baby's father. Something she should have done in the first place. Ben was going to tan her hide.

Jacob ran his hands over his unshaved face. His palms rasped across the stubble. Should he confront her and lead her back home or let her come back after she was safely wed? What did he know about the Woods family?

There were a lot of them. Ten under one roof. All the children, except for John, attended Jacob's school in dirty, patched clothing. One thing was for certain—Viola wasn't bettering her station in life. A pity, with her looks. She'd most likely have three or four babies by the time she turned twenty. Mind made up, Jacob stood and stepped into the clearing.

Viola and John whirled. John grabbed a nearby hog's leg shotgun and aimed it at Jacob's chest. "State your business, teacher."

"I've come to take Viola home." Jacob took care to keep his hands in the open.

"I'm not going home, Mr. Wright." Viola lifted her pretty chin. "They hate me there."

"No, they don't. It's all a big misunderstanding. Come home and let your Pa help you with your burdens."

She narrowed her eyes and folded her hands over her stomach. "You calling my baby a burden?"

"You just turned seventeen."

John shifted his gun. "My ma will help."

"You ma has her hands full." Jacob took a step forward.

"Stop." John shook his head. "You don't know anything, mister. You come in here with your city ways and try to tell us how to live, what to learn, how to talk. Stealing our women. Trying to turn us from our way of life." He pulled the trigger.

The bullet kicked up the dirt at Jacob's feet.

Viola screamed and stepped in front of John. "Don't shoot him. Enough has been done on my account. Mr. Wright, tell my sister that I'm sorry, and we'll be back in a day or two." She took John's arm and led the young man in the opposite direction.

Jacob had no choice but to let them go. He added another failure to his long list. How was he going to tell the Lillie family one of their own had flown the coop? He kicked at a rock, scuffing his new boot. Fitting.

Shoulders slumped, he made his way back to the mule and climbed onto the animal's back. He might as well finish his trip to Dixon's place. He needed to purchase a few items to take to the homes of his students when he started his weekly visits.

A proud people, he'd have to be careful what he took. Coffee, maybe. A tin of biscuits. Nothing that would make a big difference in any of their lives, but might possibly give them a taste of something finer in life.

John's words about Jacob trying to change the hill folk drifted through his mind. He didn't want to change anyone. Was there anything wrong with wanting to show the people that there were other things available to them than backbreaking poverty or money earned by making and selling whiskey?

He glanced at the scudding clouds overhead. *Lord, help me help these people without offending.* Too much harm had already been done.

*

"Where is that girl?" Grandma turned from the sink of dirty dishes and waved a wooden spoon in Phoebe's direction. "She knows she's got to pick up the slack while you're ailing."

Ailing? Phoebe snorted, not glancing up from her quilting. She didn't give one whit about where her no-good sister had gone to. She jabbed the needle through the fabric and into her finger.

Hissing, she stuck the injured appendage into her mouth and eyed the shotgun hanging in its place above the fireplace. She still wanted to shoot Eli. She didn't reckon that feeling would go away anytime soon. But she didn't want to shoot her sister. Slap her, maybe, or pull her hair.

"She's probably off sulking because I wouldn't forgive her for her loose tongue." Phoebe checked her finger to make sure it wasn't bleeding before picking her needle back up.

Grandma nodded. "She's got to learn that tears don't always make everything better."

The front door banged open, and Pa barged in. "Where's Viola?"

Heart in her throat, Phoebe jumped to her feet. "Grandma and I were discussing the very thing. We don't know. What's happened?"

"The oldest Wood boy is gone, too." Pa sighed. "That girl will be the death of me. I'll skin her hide to where she can't sit for a week."

"She's a woman grown, Ben." Grandma pointed at his seat at the head of the table. "Eat. She'll turn up."

"Like a bad penny." Pa's chair scraped across the floor. He glanced at Phoebe. "Aren't you going to eat?"

"I already did. You were out so early this morning, we've all finished." She moved to the next square in her quilt. Usually, the repetitive motions soothed her. Not today. All she saw in every stitch was Eli's drunken sneer.

The quilt, aptly named *An Old Maid's Ramble*, was sure to be a beauty and should fetch a good price at the spring fair. After falling for Jacob, Phoebe had almost hoped this quilt would be the last she made until after stitching one to go on her marriage bed. Fitting how this one should haunt her. She'd be an old maid for sure.

The fact she hadn't seen Jacob in a while,

confirmed the fact he only courted her to get close to the moonshiners. That man had a hard hankering to right some wrong. Well, he wasn't going to use Phoebe to do it. Tears clogged her throat. Regardless of how she felt about him, it was best to let him move on and find a woman worthy of him. She'd tell him as soon as she could face looking at a man other than Pa.

The way she was now, just the thought of a man laying eyes on her, much less touching her, made her stomach roil. What kind of a wife would she make now? She clapped a hand over her mouth. What if she carried Eli's baby in her womb? She cast a startled glance at Pa. He'd commit murder for sure.

Ma's voice drifted from beyond the grave, telling her not to borrow trouble, for the day had enough of its own. That was a certainty.

A knock on the door sent Phoebe scurrying into the bedroom she shared with her Grandma and sisters. True to Grandma's word, the boys had been sent to the loft and the girls given the bedroom. Phoebe left the bedroom door open enough to peer out of.

"I'll get it." Pa clutched his rifle and swung the door open.

A very battered Eli stood, hat in one hand, flowers in the other, on the porch. "I've come to ask Phoebe to be my wife." He held up the hand holding the flowers. "Hear me out, Ben. I know I did her wrong, but I was in a drunken stupor and not in full capacity of my senses. Surely, you believe that."

"The only thing I know is that you are asking for me to put a bullet in your gut." Pa jammed him with the rifle.

Phoebe's hands shook as she clutched the doorframe. She wanted to dash out and scream that Eli was the last man on earth she'd ever want to marry. There was no longer any need for pretense. He'd ruined her. There was nothing left for her but to stay behind and raise her siblings. That and help Pa bring down the ring of moonshiners. She couldn't help but feel a bit of pleasure knowing that could also result in Eli's demise. Marry him? She'd rot in hell first.

Tears streamed down her cheeks, and she plopped onto the bed. Had she given up all hope in her Heavenly Father as well as her hope in finding a husband? Possibly. Why would God let Eli take the one thing Phoebe had of any worth?

"Phoebe." Pa yelled from the front room. "You want to marry this skunk."

"No! I'd rather see him dead." She buried her face in her hands.

"Then I suspect you'd best skedaddle, Eli."

"You're threatening the wrong man," Eli said. "I might have made a mistake, but I've come to apologize. That's the Christian thing to do, just as it's the Christian way for y'all to forgive me. Don't forget I got powerful friends. People that will side with me if it comes down to the two of us. It don't make one bit of difference to any of them that you're in this gang with us."

"Get the hell off my property, Eli. That's the last warning you'll get."

The door slammed. Phoebe released a shuddering breath as a new plan formed in her mind.

15

Jacob entered Dixon's store. Five heads turned to glare at him. What unimagined slight had he done now? He nodded. "Folks." Not one person returned his greeting. A chill ran down his spine that had nothing to do with winter.

Dixon stood behind the counter, his normally cheerful face dour. "What can I do for you, Mr. Wright?"

"He's here to stir up more trouble," one of the men in front of the potbellied stove, said. "He ought to go back where he came from."

The others nodded.

Jacob frowned. "I'm confused, gentlemen. Have I slighted you in some way?"

"You slighted Eli Coffman. You slight one of us, you slight us all." More head nodding.

Jacob had to bite his tongue not to blurt out the truth of the man's evil. "We had a gentleman's understanding regarding the courting of Phoebe Lillie. I'm sorry if Eli feels cheated."

"It's been understood that Eli and Phoebe would get hitched for a couple of years," the man said, spitting into a nearby spittoon. "Until you moseyed into our hollow."

"I honestly don't believe Phoebe intended to marry Eli. That was all in Eli's head." Not having anticipated a store full of angry hill folk, he was no longer in a gift-buying mood. After purchasing the items he needed personally, Jacob headed back into the watery afternoon sun.

He pulled the collar of his jacket around his neck, and shivered. The temperature was dropping with every hour. Hopefully, Viola and her beau would hit town before snow fell.

He turned the mule toward the Lillie place. Someone had to let them know that Viola had run off. Otherwise, Phoebe would worry, and Jacob couldn't let another hardship rest on her shoulders.

When he spotted Eli shuffling in his direction, Jacob was tempted to pull into the trees instead of facing the man. But, he'd chosen to stop running from the unpleasant things of life, and halted in the middle of the road instead. If life could go on after Jacob was responsible for a woman's death, he figured he could handle an ornery cuss like Eli. He tightened his hold on the reins to keep from sliding from the mule's back and punching the man.

Eli dragged his feet, head down, not seeming to care that he staggered across the road. Had he been drinking? His love of the whiskey he helped make and sell was what caused him to hurt Phoebe. That and the man's foolish pride.

"Morning, Eli." Jacob narrowed his eyes, searching to see whether the man had a weapon. Not seeing one, he relaxed his hold a bit on the reins.

"I reckon you're pleased with yourself." Eli glared, crossing his arms. "Seems Phoebe is done with me." His lips thinned in a sneer. "But maybe she's done with all men now."

Jacob shoved the old enemy rage deep inside. He thought he'd left that emotion behind when he quit law enforcement. Now, heat rose up his neck, calling his name. His fingers itched to clamp around the pistol in his waistband. There were no innocents to get in the way, no one to know other than the evil man who needed to be stopped. And Jacob. The thought left a bitter taste in his mouth. Even with the almost consuming desire to take Eli down, he knew taking the other man's life would wound God, and that was something Jacob couldn't do.

"Cat caught your tongue, Teacher or are you afraid to stand up to a real man?"

"When I see a real man, I'll let you know." He clicked the reins and moved past Eli.

The man's taunts hung in the cold air like a fog, choking Jacob's spirit. The skin on his back tightened, expecting an ambush. When he reached the turnoff to the Lillie place, he relaxed. But he wasn't fool enough to believe that Eli wouldn't make an attempt to harm him should the opportunity arise.

The Lillie's hound barked a welcome when Jacob stopped in front of the house. The front door opened and Ben stepped out, sawed off shotgun in hand. "Howdy, Jacob. Thought you might be Eli Coffman come to stir up more trouble."

Jacob slid to the ground. "I passed him half a mile back." From the murderous look on Ben's face, the other man's visit hadn't been a pleasant one. "How's Phoebe?"

"Fine, but she ain't up for company."

"I figured as much." Only time and God's love would heal what ailed Phoebe. Jacob would have to be patient. "Do you have a minute to talk?"

Ben nodded and motioned to the steps. "What's on your mind?"

Jacob sat next to him, hands hanging between his knees. "I'm in quandary about how to get through to these mountain people. You know them. What am I doing wrong? They've taken sides between me and Eli and I've come out the loser."

"They still sending their young'uns to school?"

Jacob nodded. "I want to help the families as a whole. Not just book learning for the children."

"That, my friend." Ben clapped him on the shoulder. "Will take time. Eli was born and raised in this hollow."

"But he's bringing evil here."

"He brings money. Something these people have very little of." Ben picked up a stone from beside his scuffed boot and tossed it skittering across the ground. "Still, I'm hoping to put a stop to it all, even at the risk of turning my neighbors against me. The problem is … I don't think Eli is the boss man. There's someone higher up I'm trying to draw out."

"What can I do?" Jacob shivered against the cold and hooked the top button on his coat. Ben's fervor against the moonshiners filled the air like a frigid wind. Lots of mountain people brewed the stuff. Why was Ben so set against it? Why didn't he just warn his family to stay away and mind their own business? Much like Jacob wished he could. The law was the law, and obviously Ben had morals despite his simple upbringing.

He bit his tongue to keep from blurting out the many questions. "I used to be in law enforcement. I might have connections that will help."

Ben shook his head. "Not yet, and keep your past job a secret if you value your hide. Let's find out who is top of command, and then, if you still want to help, we'll make our plan."

*

Phoebe let the faded curtain fall into place. She wasn't sure her plan would work if Jacob joined their efforts. The man might carry a gun, but it was as plain as the mountain that he was afraid to use it.

The man. Tears stung Phoebe's eyes. Eli had taken more than her virtue, he'd taken her heart. Jacob, the man she loved was now delegated to two words.

She eyed the rifle over the fireplace. She'd reclaim what was lost or die trying.

"Planning to commit murder?" Grandma lowered into her rocking chair and picked up a pair of coveralls that needed mending.

"I might." Phoebe pulled a cane-seated chair up to her quilting frame.

"Don't say as I blame you much, but it won't set a good example for your siblings, nor will it make God smile."

Phoebe picked up her needle and jammed it through the top layer through to the bottom. Grandma was right, but Phoebe couldn't change the way she felt. "Eli took the only thing of worth I had to give a husband. I aim to make him pay."

"You have your love to give, child." Grandma narrowed her eyes. "There's always that. If you're thinking Jacob Wright won't want you anymore, then maybe you're right. Maybe you aren't fit for a fine man like that."

Her head shot up, and she locked gazes with her grandmother. "That's a cruel thing to say."

Grandma shrugged. "Sometimes the truth

hurts."

"But what if I can't give a man my love any longer? What if I can't bring myself to let a man … touch me? What if I can't perform my … duties?" Phoebe swallowed back the tears clogging her throat.

"A man who loves you, well, his touch will make you forget all that. Trust your old grandma." A smile spread across her weathered face. "I still have a bit of wisdom left in this old body of mine. Why don't you go outside and check on the young'uns? They're quiet, which means they're up to no good."

Phoebe slipped the needle into the quilt fabric and headed outside, thankful Jacob and Pa weren't in sight. By the time she reached the barn, the children's voices reached her ears. Her heart sank not hearing Viola's. Where had that girl gone to?

"Now, this is what we're gonna do." JJ traced in the dirt with a stick. "The babies won't be any help, but us boys are going to head up to that still and set fire to the shack. Pa needs all the help he can get, and I aim to give it to him."

"You will not." Phoebe grabbed her brother by the collar and yanked him to his feet, not caring that he stood several inches taller than herself. "You want to get yourself killed?" She glared at each of the little ones. "You let Pa and me handle this."

"You?" JJ yanked free and crossed his arms.

159

"You're nothing but a girl."

"Get in the house." Phoebe pointed and watched as all but JJ dashed away. "You want to be a man? Then don't take children to do a grownup's job." She grabbed the hog's leg from where her brother had leaned it against the barn siding and shoved it at him. "Make a plan. Talk with Pa. Don't run off willy-nilly to get killed."

Once JJ stormed off, Phoebe leaned against the barn wall and closed her eyes. What was happening to their happy hollow? What evil had someone brought into their midst? An evil that threatened children and tore families apart? Thankful Pa had seemed fit to come out of hiding and tend to his family, Phoebe knew she still had a part to play in it all.

The question was—what would happen to her when she followed through? There were only two outcomes. One was success, the other death.

The deep rumble of men's voices drifted around the corner, and Phoebe scooted into the sanctuary of the barn. When would she feel safe enough to face Jacob and not fear the pity she'd see in his eyes?

Her life now had more questions than answers, and her soul had a rift she didn't think could be healed. She glanced at the high-raftered ceiling above her head. Was God there for her anymore? How could He be when her heart held such bitterness and despair?

Always the strong sister, the weakness that drowned her frightened her. She hadn't been awake for Eli's assault, yet darkness engulfed her, making it hard to breathe. Ma would have told her to seek counsel, but now that Pine Ridge didn't have a permanent pastor, who could Phoebe talk to? Certainly not Jacob. He'd once told her he preached on occasion, but part of her despair concerned him. She couldn't.

Grandma was wise, but she would tell Phoebe everything would work out in time. Phoebe might not have a lot of time left. She had decided to put her plan into action the next time Pa headed up the mountain. If he said no, she'd go herself.

The hollow had to get back to normal before all was lost.

16

A fternoon, Sheriff." Pa's voice rang across the yard.

Phoebe peeked out of the barn to see the middle-aged man with a paunch saunter across their yard. Sheriff Johnson might come up from Compton once in a while to establish law and order, but something about the way the man leered at every female in sight always put Phoebe's nerves on edge.

"Ben." Sheriff Johnson removed his hat and propped one foot on a sawed off stump. "I'm here to speak to your Viola." His gaze flicked to Jacob.

The sheriff wasn't saying everything he needed to say. Phoebe could see it in the way his eyes shifted across the yard, always settling on Jacob. She moved to the barn opening.

"Why's that?" Pa squared his shoulders. "She done something wrong?"

The sheriff shook his head. "I don't know. The Woods family is looking for their eldest boy, and they seem to think he might be with Viola."

"We haven't seen Viola since yesterday." Pa squared his shoulders. "I'm sure she ran off with that boy."

Jacob stepped forward. "She did, Ben."

What was he saying? Disregarding the fact she would be surrounded by men, Phoebe shuffled forward and stood just behind her pa.

"When I was headed to Dixon's, I saw Viola duck into the woods. I followed her and was run off, at gunpoint, by John Wood. They were headed to the city to get married." He directed his attention to the sheriff. "You probably passed them in Compton. I'm sorry, Ben."

Pa shook his head. "No apology necessary. Viola is my wild one. I never could control her. Well," he hitched his rifle higher. "If she don't come back wed to that whelp, I'll make sure they get hitched. You tell the Woods family that."

Sheriff Johnson nodded. "I'll tell them. There's something else I've driven up here for and that's to talk to the teacher. I'm glad I found him here."

"Sheriff?" Jacob frowned.

"Seems I've had some complaints about you meddling in people's private affairs." The sheriff's lips stretched to a thin line in his ruddy face. "And Eli Coffman said you accosted him on the road."

"I did no such thing." Jacob crossed his arms. "The man made threats and taunted me until I was out of sight. I never got off my mule."

The screen door squawked. Phoebe glanced over her shoulder to see JJ step outside, his dark eyes wide. She motioned for him to go back inside, but he shook his head and glared. Fine. Foolish boy. Pa could deal with him.

"Still," the sheriff said. "I have to give you a warning to stay away from Eli."

Phoebe rushed forward. "Pa, tell the sheriff what Eli did to me." Heat infused her face. "The man needs to go to jail."

Sheriff Johnson removed his hat and ran his fingers along the brim, not meeting Phoebe's eyes. "The way Eli tells it, you came on to him while taking a walk in the woods."

The lie strengthened Phoebe's resolve to do something. "He's a bald-faced liar, and I aim to make him pay." She whirled, twisting her knee and tried to march into the house without showing pain.

Inside, she stormed to the bedroom, yelled at her sisters to leave, and then slammed the door. She threw herself face down on the bed, not caring that she acted like a child. Sometimes tears and tantrums were all that would make a girl feel better. Ever since Ma died, Phoebe had been the strong one. The person who was there to pick up the slack. Now, she ached with a pain that weighed upon her, filled her with anger, an emotion she had previously had little experience with.

She rolled over, and stared at the ceiling. Tears rolled down her face, soaking into her braids. She wanted to feel God's presence again. She wanted Him to take away the hurtful feelings that wounded her. She wanted life to go back the way it was. But, she was old enough to know that a person didn't always get what they want.

Jacob's voice, raised in anger, drifted through the thin wall, and her heart ached a little more. Last week, Phoebe had thought she'd found her husband. Now, she was resigned to being an old maid. Nothing more than a castoff.

If Pa didn't marry the widow Williams, Phoebe would spend the next few years raising her siblings, never to have children of her own. If Pa did marry, where would that leave Phoebe? Maybe she could stay here and care for Grandma while Pa moved into the widow's place.

A draft blew through the boards forming the rooms walls, and she rolled up in the quilt, feeling very much like a swaddling baby. Through the closed door came Grandma and the children's murmurs as they pitched in to help with supper.

Someone banged on the door. "Grandma said come help!" Callie's voice pierced Phoebe's fog. "You've pouted around enough. If you don't start doing something your bones will freeze up and you'll be an old lady."

Phoebe groaned and unrolled from the warm blanket. She was already an old lady. She opened the door and stepped into the toasty front room.

"About time." Grandma shoved a wooden spoon in her hand. "Finish up this stew and make some biscuits. My feet are killing me."

"Yes, ma'am." Phoebe stirred the flour and milk in the bowl.

"I don't want no more moping around." Grandma poked the fire with a stick. "Enough is enough. You're a strong girl. Act like it."

Oh, she intended to at the first opportunity. Only retaliation would ease the burning in her heart. She smiled without humor, anticipating Eli's face when she made him pay.

For a second, the faces of his children flashed across her mind. They'd be orphaned if something happened to Eli. She shook her head. He had family farther up the mountain that would care for them.

*

"That's insane." Jacob shoved his hands in his pockets to stop their trembling. "Your kids need you here, not traipsing off up the mountain." Ben had his priorities wrong. He needed to be at home and let the law handle the moonshiners.

"I have to get back to work before someone grows suspicious."

"What if the authorities find the still while

you're working? You'll go to jail, Ben."

"That's a risk I've got to take. Besides, son, you need to trust me. Tomorrow, I got a few men going up with me to wreck those moonshine trucks. Once we do that, we all have to go into hiding for a while." He laid a hand on Jacob's shoulder. "I'm counting on you to look after my brood. Will you?"

"You know I will." Jacob rubbed his hands through his hair. "I'm sorry I didn't immediately tell you about Viola, but she's seventeen now and I figured her business was hers. I would've told you if I thought you were worrying."

Ben waved off his apology. "I know my daughter. No apology necessary. Are you afraid to use that gun on your hip?"

"No, I choose not to." Leaning against the porch railing, Jacob watched the sun set over the mountain. He loved this hollow and its people, one in particular, and couldn't think of living anywhere else. More than anything, he wanted this whole horrible moonshine mess to end so he could convince Phoebe she belonged with him, and that Eli's actions had nothing to do with how he felt about her.

"During my days as law enforcement, my partner and I responded to a domestic disturbance. A man held a gun to his wife's head. He was drunk beyond all reason. Five children watched from the window as we told him to relinquish his gun." Jacob took a deep shuddering breath, the memory like a knife in his gut.

"Even with all my training, it was the first time I'd had to draw my gun on a man. The husband cocked the gun. The children were crying. Silent tears ran down the wife's face." Jacob could see it as plain as if the scene took place in front of him at that moment. His eyes burned. "I gave him one more directive, then took the shot. At that moment, the man yanked his wife in front of him. The bullet went through her into him, killing them both and leaving a handful of orphans. I told myself at that time, I'd never draw on another human. It still haunts my sleep."

It wasn't until that moment that he saw Phoebe's pale face come around the corner of the house. Her shocked expression told him she'd heard all, or at least most, of his story. Instead of anger or disgust, he saw pity flit across her features. The one emotion he wanted least to see.

"It wasn't your fault," Ben said. "It could have happened to anyone. Evil exists in this world. That's why me and the others want to put a stop to it, at least in Pine Ridge. You're a fine, Godly man. You'll do what's right when the time comes."

Jacob wasn't so sure. What if someone had Phoebe or another member of the Lillie family in their sights? Could he shoot to save them or would he freeze as solid as a pond in deep winter?

"Supper's ready." Phoebe brushed past them and headed back into the house, avoiding Jacob's gaze.

"Stay for supper?" Ben turned to follow his daughter.

Although it would most likely stick in his throat, Jacob nodded and moved inside. They'd already set him a place at the table, and he squeezed in between Ben and JJ. The rich aroma of beef and vegetables swimming in gravy teased his nostrils. The fire warmed his back. For the first time in a long time, Jacob felt part of a family. What would happen if Ben didn't return? Would the Lillie's become his family because of a lack of a man around the house? He didn't want Phoebe to marry him out of obligation. He wanted her undying love.

"I'm going to be gone for a while," Ben said, digging into his stew. "Jacob is going to stay here while I'm gone. Y'all respect his authority, you hear?"

"No disrespect, but I'm old enough to care for the family," JJ spoke up. "This ain't the first time you've headed somewhere."

Phoebe's gaze darted from Ben to Jacob. "But this time, you might not return, right? What are you planning?"

"Nothing you need to worry about. Just help your grandma." Ben dipped a biscuit into his gravy. "I'll be back."

"I'm going with you," she said.

"No, you're not." Ben pointed a finger at her. "I'll lock you in your room if I have to. What I'm fixin' to do ain't for a girl."

Wonderful. Jacob would be hard pressed to keep Phoebe in line if she wanted to do something. The gleam in her eye alerted him she already had a plan up her sleeve.

After supper, Jacob and Ben moved back to the porch so Ben could smoke his pipe. They both took seats on the top step. "Ben, why are you so against the moonshine ring anyway? How does it affect you personally to where you'll risk everything to shut it down?"

There had to be more than just a moral obligation. Everything was on the line. Ben's life, and possibly the lives of his family.

"Whiskey ruined my pa and sent my brother to an early grave." He struck a match and held it to the bowl of his pipe before puffing a few times to ignite the tobacco. "I had a bit of trouble with drinking myself when I was in the army. Wasn't until I about got myself killed because I didn't have my wits about me, that I quit cold turkey." He tapped his pipe. "I don't want the evils around my family or kin. It's as simple as that. I've seen the drink ruin families. You know what it did to Phoebe."

Jacob stared across the dark yard. "Eli Coffman did that to Phoebe."

"Because of the drink. I'm going to stop that and make all those involved pay before it completely destroys my family."

17

Phoebe stepped into the kitchen as Grandma sprinkled water on spilled salt. She pressed her lips together and shook her head. When would Grandma give up on her silly superstitions? "Afraid someone will have a quarrel today?"

"Just making sure they don't." Grandma wiped the wet salt into her hand and brushed it into the sink.

"Where's Pa?" Phoebe grabbed a dry biscuit from a basket on the table and slathered on Muscadine jelly.

"Said he had business up the mountain and not to wait up for him. He said he'd be gone for a while."

Phoebe knew what that meant. Pa had gone to stop the moonshiners. To stop Eli. Not without her, he wouldn't. "I'll check on the little ones." She grabbed her sweater and dashed outside, making a beeline to the shed where she'd hidden a shotgun the day before.

The mounds of sugar bags were gone. How could she have slept through what had to be several men carting off pounds and pounds of sugar? She grabbed the shotgun and turned, running into JJ.

"Where are you going?" He asked.

"Hunting."

"For Pa and the moonshiners, I bet." He quirked his mouth. "I know where they went, but if you want me to tell you, then you have to let me go with you."

She glanced at the ax in his hand. "You don't have a gun."

"Pa took an axe."

Phoebe bit her bottom lip. She'd bet her last dollar that Pa also had his hog leg with him. What did he want an axe for? She glanced at the house, relieved to see the children playing on the porch. She didn't need them wanting to follow, too. "Fine. You can come, but stay out of my way and do what I say."

He grabbed a bag from the side of the shed. "I knew you'd let me so I brought lunch."

"Smart aleck." Phoebe hefted the gun and pushed through the thick trees by their cabin. Just as she dropped the last branch back into place, she spotted Jacob approaching the porch. Her heart raced, remembering Pa telling him to keep a watch out for her. Obviously, he'd arrived to share their cabin for the next few days. "We need to hurry."

They picked up their pace, trying to remain as quiet as possible despite their haste. Every scamper of tiny feet through the forest floor sent Phoebe's heart into overdrive. Every squawk of a bird made her skittish. What was she doing? She wasn't a vigilante. She was nothing more than a crippled quilt-making girl from the hollow.

The pale face of her younger brother gave her pause. "Maybe you should go back."

He shook his head hard enough to send a curl flopping forward over his forehead. "Not a chance. Pa might need us. Are we heading for the still?"

"You know about the still?" Why was Phoebe the last to know of something so detrimental to her family's livelihood?

"Everybody does."

Phoebe shrugged. "If Pa isn't there, we'll continue to the mountain road. The moonshiners have to be moving their product somehow, and that's the easiest way I can figure." She scrambled across a fallen tree over a swift moving creek until reaching the solid embankment on the other side.

JJ ran across like a mountain goat. Even with her improved shoe, Phoebe would never have her brother's agility.

Voices raised in anger and the rumble of engines, drove her forward. She clutched the rifle like a life line and peered through another stand of brush.

Pa and several of their neighbors stood with assorted guns and axes in hand while facing Eli and two men armed with shotguns. Behind them stood a truck filled with barrels of what could only be moonshine.

Her hands sweated and she transferred the rifle from one hand to the other, wiping her palms on her dress. Clouds, pregnant with rain, covered the sun and cast the forest into a grey afternoon. A wind blew chills up Phoebe's legs and neck. She glanced at her brother who stood as still as one of the thick tree trunks. "Afraid?"

The panic in his eyes belied the bravado of his shake of his head. "Pa needs us."

"Not us, JJ." Phoebe put a hand on his shoulder. "It isn't too late for you to go home."

"As the next oldest male in our home, I should help."

He took his role as first-born son too seriously. Maybe it was a mistake to allow him to follow. Phoebe was the one who wanted revenge. JJ had no stake in what might happen that day. "You really should go home. If something happens to me or Pa, Grandma and the younger ones will need you. We can't all go rushing in like fools."

"Fools adequately describes the two of you." A hand spun Phoebe around, and she came face-to-face with Jacob.

"Get out of here." She yanked free. "This

doesn't concern you."

"Since your Pa asked me to watch out for you, I think it does." Jacob narrowed his eyes.

She snorted. "How can you protect us? You're afraid to draw that pistol on your hip."

Pain flashed across his face. She regretted the words the moment they left her mouth, but squelched the regret deep into the recesses of her soul. There was no time for compassion. She had a job to do and nothing, or no one, would stand in her way.

*

Jacob stared into the eyes of the woman he loved and saw a stranger. Where had the soft Phoebe gone? Lost in one act of violence. His fingers itched to curl around the handle of his gun. But, he couldn't. He'd made an oath. To do so, would put him in a dangerous place: A place that could steal his soul.

She pushed him back and parted the bushes, stepping to her Pa's side. Ben turned, a muscle twitching in his jaw. "Take them away."

"I can't short of shooting them." Jacob joined the crowd facing the moonshiners. "They both snuck out before I arrived at your place." All he could do now was join the madness and pray no one was hurt or killed.

"JJ, step back by those trees. There by the water and stay out of the way." Ben squared his shoulders.

"Daughter, I'll deal with you when we get home. Jacob, keep her out of the way."

"I deserve to be here." Phoebe stomped her foot. "You can't make me leave. I snuck off and found you, therefore, I should stay."

"You brought your brother into danger. That is something I cannot tolerate." Ben's low voice should have been a warning. Even Jacob knew the man was reaching his boiling point.

He wrapped his arms around Phoebe's waist and lifted her off her feet. "Let's go by JJ. Leave these men to fight their battle."

"Let me go." She kicked and screamed like a she-cat, connecting with his shins a couple of times, until he spread his legs and walked like a bow-legged sailor to a safe distance. The men prepared to do battle laughed, momentarily pulled away from their feud.

"Calm down or I'll tie you to a tree with my belt."

"You wouldn't dare." She pummeled his chest with her fists.

He staggered back against the trunk of a tree before gathering her hands in his. "I made a promise to Ben. Please don't make me renege on that promise."

Her shoulders sagged, and she covered her face with her hands. "He's right there. Eli is standing there taunting me. Forgive me, Lord, but I want to see the light fade from the man's eyes as he takes his last breath."

"I'm sorry." Jacob gathered her in his arms and pulled her close. He rested his chin on the top of her soft head and closed his eyes, wanting nothing more than to whisk her away from the hollow and give her a better life. One where shotguns and moonshine weren't a daily occurrence. If she said the word, he'd marry her and cart her off to Little Rock.

By this time, Ben and his group charged past the three moonshiners. They raised their axes and the woods reverberated with the sound of metal on metal. Moonshine filled the air with its stench.

Jacob's grip on Phoebe eased. Along with JJ they watched in awe as the men tore the trucks and barrels to shreds, and the ground soaked with hundreds of dollars' worth of illegal whiskey.

"Wow." JJ stepped from under the overhang of an oak. "Pa is really serious about shutting this down. I want to be a part of it."

Phoebe shot out an arm to stop him. "No. They are handling things just fine."

The moonshiners entered the fray, yanking men from the truck and throwing punches. Two of them propped their rifles against a boulder while Eli stood back and rolled a homemade cigarette.

Jacob was astounded at the man's coolness. Did he have no conscience? No remorse for his deeds?

Phoebe shuddered next to him, and Jacob put his arm around her shoulders. She stiffened, but didn't pull away. Maybe they could repair their love after all? Given time, once the moonshiners were put away and Eli dealt with, she would see how much Jacob still cared for her. He'd make sure of it.

"That's enough." Eli blew a smoke ring into the air. "Y'all have had your fun." He lifted his rifle and shot into the sky.

The men grappling around the trucks turned. Ben took two steps forward. "We aren't finished until you bunch of no-gooders are run out of this hollow."

Eli dropped his smoke and ground it into the leaves under his feet. "Don't provoke me, Ben. I have ways of hurting you that you can't even comprehend."

"We'd call the sheriff," Ben said. "But I'm guessing he's in cahoots with you."

Eli shrugged. "So you take your self-righteousness here to where I provide for my family and try to take that all away from me. Not everyone has an army pension to help make ends meet." He aimed the barrel at Ben's chest.

Phoebe made a move to dash forward, and Jacob grabbed her arm. "Don't. You'll distract your pa."

A rustle in the brush behind them drew Jacob's attention. He turned and peered, unable to make out anything in the thickness. Most likely an animal disturbed by all the ruckus.

"Want me to check it out?" JJ asked. "It's better than standing here doing nothing while the rest of the men are fighting to save our livelihood."

"Don't leave," Phoebe said. "I don't want you out of my sight."

"I'm not a child." He glared into the trees. "I think I saw something." He parted the branches of an overgrown pine tree.

A shot rang out.

JJ's eyes widened and he pitched forward.

Jacob jumped to grab him, the boy's shirt slipping through his fingers.

JJ fell into the murky creek and disappeared under the swift moving water.

18

Jacob kicked off his shoes and splashed into the creek, ignoring the fight that erupted with an all new fury behind him with more shots being fired. Phoebe screamed and raced up and down the bank as Jacob fought the current and dove time after time to find JJ.

The bitter bite of the freezing water stole his breath yet he continued to search for the boy, praying he'd find him before it was too late. He didn't think the Lillie family would survive the loss of Ben's oldest boy.

Soon, Ben and a few of his group, Jacob hoped they weren't all that was left of the fighters, thundered down the bank ahead of him. Precious minutes ticked by, and Jacob found nothing but weeds and rocks.

"Find my boy!" Ben shouted, his breath pluming from his mouth like dragon fire. "Please, God, save him."

Jacob's fingers and toes burned with the cold,

yet he didn't give up. Wait. There. His fingers grasped fabric and he pulled, ripping JJ away from the submerged tree branches. "Here. I can't get him out myself."

Eager hands lifted the boy from Jacob's arms, and then helped Jacob up the bank. He collapsed on his back, shivering and gasping.

"He isn't breathing." Phoebe fell to her knees beside her brother. "Jacob?"

With what strength he had left, he rolled to his side to face her. "Help me up. I'm frozen."

Ben held out a hand and hauled Jacob to his feet. "Can you save him?"

"I'll try." During his time on the force, he'd witnessed a man breathe life into a drowning victim. He sent up a swift prayer that he could do the same.

Blood spread across JJ's chest, staining his denim overalls despite his soaking in the creek. Jacob knelt and tilted the boy's head, then felt for a pulse. Nothing. He breathed in twice, and then pressed ten times on JJ's chest. The boy's pallor made him work faster despite the pain in his body from his own dunking. After the fifth sequence of breathe and press, JJ coughed. Jacob rolled him on his side so the boy could vomit, then collapsed and closed his eyes.

When he opened his eyes, he lay in the largest bed in the Lillie home next to JJ. A man hovered over them pressing a stethoscope to JJ's chest. He turned and smiled when Jacob tried to sit.

"You're a hero, Mr. Wright. From what I hear, you saved this young man's life. I'm Doctor Riley, and I'm pleased to make your acquaintance."

"Likewise." Jacob slung his legs over the side of the bed and wrapped the quilt around his shoulders. "I can't get warm."

"Water's mighty cold this time of year. You were in it for a few minutes."

"How's JJ?"

The doctor frowned. "We'll know in a day or two. I got the bullet out and stitched him up. Now, we worry about infection and pneumonia. You should take care of yourself, too."

"Where is everyone?" The house was unusually quiet. Even with Jacob in the back bedroom, he should be able to hear chatter from the family.

"I sent them out to the porch until I checked the two of you over." The doctor stashed his equipment in a black leather bag. "With all the wailing and commotion, I couldn't hear myself think. I'll send them in, but I want you to rest for the next couple of days. You're at risk of pneumonia, too."

Jacob nodded. Sleep for the next week sounded good to him. He lay back, making sure JJ was covered before he rolled up in his own blanket and closed his eyes.

"Mr. Wright?" Grandma patted his cheek. "I

made you some chicken soup. Can you sit up and eat it while it's hot?"

"I'd like to eat at the table if that's all right." He wasn't an invalid, just tired and cold.

Her wrinkled face beamed. "Why that would be fine. I've got hot coffee, too. We'll have you warmed up in no time."

Ben met him at the door, tears in his eyes, and lifted Jacob's arm around his shoulders. "Whatever you need. Just say the word."

"I'm not an invalid for starters." He never was a man for others groveling at his feet. He'd done what needed doing. Anyone would have.

"Let us wait on you. You gave us a gift we can never repay." Ben helped him to the head of the table. "I bet you were a great lawman."

Hardly. Jacob glanced at the expectant faces around the table. All but one. Phoebe stared at her lap. Even after the drenching, the shooting, the saving, she still hung back, not wanting to have anything to do with him. He sat in the chair pulled out for him.

"What happened after I passed out? Who was killed?"

Ben took his seat. "One of my group, two of Eli's. Unfortunately, Eli wasn't one of them. Who shot my boy?"

Jacob shook his head. "The shot came from the trees behind us. Someone was hiding. JJ parted the branches and was shot. That's all I know."

Ben picked up the sharp knife next to his plate and jammed it into the table top, the handle quivering with the force. "When my boy wakes up, he'll be able to tell us who was there. Until then, we cool our heels." He knocked on Phoebe's bent head. "You hear me, girl?"

"I hear you." She raised her head, her features cold and unyielding. "But I'll do what I've got to. Maybe you should run and hide with the widow again and let me run things here."

"I'll pretend you didn't say that." Ben yanked his knife out of the table and dropped it back down. "I'll tie you in the shed if I have to."

"What's going on?" They all turned to see Viola and John Woods. "Why are y'all eating so early in the day? Where's JJ?"

"Where in tarnation have you been?" Ben lunged to his feet and grabbed his shotgun. "What have you done?"

Viola straightened her shoulders. "I've gotten married. I'm carrying your first grandchild."

"While you've been off gallivanting around the country, you're brother lies in there dying." Ben's shoulders slumped. "You should have come to me, girl."

"You would have threatened to shoot John." Her hand slipped into her new husband's. "I wanted to let you know before we headed to the Woods property. Who shot JJ?"

"We don't know, but the teacher saved his life at the risk of his own."

Jacob squirmed under the adoring glances of Phoebe's family. He hadn't thought twice about jumping into the creek. His bones ached with cold, and it might take a month of Sundays to warm up, but he'd do it again for someone he cared about. His gaze met Phoebe's across the table.

*

It was her fault that JJ lay in the bed. She'd allowed him to follow. Jacob was a hero, doing what Phoebe couldn't. If he hadn't been there, her brother would have died. Phoebe had never been a strong swimmer because of her leg. Just one more thing to show she wasn't worthy of Jacob Wright.

Now, her soul lay as cold as the creek JJ had fallen into. Fear filled her, rushing through her veins like a sickness. She pushed back her chair and, without glancing at Viola, headed to the bedroom to check on JJ. Someday she would have to forgive her sister for her part in Phoebe's attack, but she couldn't do it now. Not with her own demons to tend.

She glanced at her unfinished quilt, raised to the roof until she was ready to once again work on it. She wasn't sure when that would be. As time passed, it became harder and harder to focus on anything of beauty.

She pulled a rocking chair into the room with JJ and took a seat before smoothing his dark hair away from his pale face. The thought of losing her younger brother brought tears to her eyes. She swallowed against the lump in her throat.

JJ groaned and opened his eyes. "Sis?"

The tears escaped, running down her face in tiny rivers. She wiped them on her shoulder and gripped her brother's hand. "How do you feel?"

"Like someone shot me. What happened?"

"Someone did shoot you, and you fell into the creek. Jacob jumped in to save you." She choked on her words. "You were dead, but he breathed life back into you. I'm so sorry I didn't force you to go home."

"That wasn't your fault, sis. You've never been able to make me do something I didn't want to do. You should marry Jacob." JJ squeezed her hand. "He's a good man."

"I'm not good enough for him." She sobbed and laid her forehead on the husk-filled mattress. "He needs someone pure and who is right with God. I'm so consumed with a thirst for revenge, that I can't think straight."

"I'll pray for you."

The thought that her brother, a boy lying at death's door, would offer to pray for such a one as she, melted the first piece of ice from her heart. Who was she to feel she could take on the sole responsibility of vengeance? Didn't God promise to take care of that for his children?

She lifted her head to see JJ had fallen back to sleep. Instead of joining the others, she stayed in his room until she dozed herself. When she woke, the sun had cast long shadows into the room, someone had placed a quilt around her shoulders, and Jacob was asleep next to JJ.

As quiet as possible, she stood and folded the quilt, placing it at the foot of the bed, and then moved to stare into Jacob's face. His dark hair was mussed. Long lashes cast shadows on his cheeks. His chiseled lips were relaxed in sleep. She wanted to tell him she still loved him, that she wanted nothing more than to be his wife, but until she found her way to forgiveness, she couldn't.

Instead, she kissed the tips of her fingers and placed them on his lips. "I love you, Jacob Wright," she whispered.

She left the room and grabbed her shawl from beside the door. Time alone in the evening cold should clear her mind. She made little noise stepping outside. Taking a seat on the top step, she glanced into the star studded sky.

"God, are you listening? I've strayed so far." She hunched over and wrapped her arms around her middle. "I've been so full of hate toward Viola and Eli. What if I carry his child in my womb? Will I be able to love it?" She sniffed against the ever present tears.

"My hatred almost got Jacob and JJ killed today, despite what they say. I should have stayed home where Pa told me to be. Then none of us would have been there. Forgive me, Father." Not only did she have to ask God for forgiveness, but Viola as well. She still thought Eli could rot in hell, but she would work on forgiving him in her heart.

A pebble rolled across the walkway and thunked against the steps. Viola stood at the edge of the property, looking almost as ethereal as a ghost in a light-colored gown. Didn't she know how dangerous it was to wander around at night in her nightclothes?

Phoebe pushed to her feet and shuffled toward her sister. She stared into Viola's tear-streaked face for a moment before holding her arms wide. With a sob, Viola rushed in until they were both sobbing. "I'm so sorry, Phoebe."

"Me, too."

"I didn't mean anything to happen. I was just mad because Jacob chose you over me. I already had this baby growing in my stomach, I just didn't know yet."

Phoebe wrapped her arms tighter. They'd taken the first step toward healing and another chunk of ice fell from her heart. "I know. I forgive you."

Viola pulled back. "How's JJ?"

"He'll be okay—" The door banged open before

her.

They whirled to see Pa standing there in his long winter underwear. "Get in the house. JJ woke up and said it was Sheriff Johnson who shot him. Viola, you're staying here tonight, you foolish girl. Tomorrow, we're going hunting."

19

Three days after his dunking, Jacob headed to Dixon's to purchase supplies for the Lillie family in return for their care. They wouldn't want to accept, on account of him saving JJ, but he'd insist. They had little to share yet fed him gladly.

The bell over Dixon's door jingled his arrival. The same two men who had glared at him the last time he'd stepped inside now grinned and rushed to pat his back.

Mr. Dixon came forward with a huge grin of his own. "There's our hero."

What strange people these hollow folk. Jacob returned the handshakes, glad he was at last accepted. "I've come for some supplies."

"Whatever you want is free of charge," Dixon announced. "Within reason, of course."

"No, I appreciate it, but I've the funds to pay. Can you let folks know that school will be starting back up on Monday?"

"Looks like snow outside. If it's too deep, students won't come, but I'll tell them." Dixon moved behind the shop counter. "What can I get you?"

"Flour, sugar, coffee, beans, some peppermint candy ..." He tapped his forefinger on his lips and studied a blue dress in the window. "Got one of those in Phoebe's size?"

"I reckon I do. You finally gonna propose to that gal?"

"I'm hoping to, when the time is right." Jacob waited while the store keeper wrapped his packages. He'd escaped a serious illness from his time in the frigid water and JJ was making steady improvement. No one had seen hide nor hair of Eli in days.

What of his children? Jacob would have to go check on them. If Eli had disappeared, they couldn't stay up on the mountain alone. He hoped someone had already thought of the children. He couldn't stand thinking they'd been alone for three days.

Back outside, he shoved his packages in bags hanging on each side of his mule, and then pulled the collar of his coat higher on his neck. It would snow for sure. Hopefully, after he returned home from checking on the Coffman children.

He guided the mule up the mountain as the first snowflakes fell. Maybe he should have stopped and let the Lillies know where he was going. What if he ended up snowbound for the night? They'd worry, even with him saying he planned on sleeping under his own roof that night.

The Coffman cabin sat lopsided on the side of the mountain. Smoke curled from the chimney. At least the children were warm. "Hello, the house!" Jacob rested his hand on the butt of his gun and prayed he wouldn't have to draw.

"What do you want?" A hunched over old woman in threadbare clothes answered the door.

"I'm the teacher, Mr. Wright. I've come to check on the children since their Pa is away. Is everything all right?" A raw-boned hound brayed from the side of the house, keeping Jacob on the back of the mule.

"As good as not having our hunter with us can make us." The woman started to close the door.

Jacob thought of the supplies in his pack. "Could you use some flour? A bit of canned meat?"

"We don't cotton to charity."

"You can pay me back when times are better."

"Times don't get better around here." She slammed the door.

Surely the folks who had once stood by Eli would now stand by his family. What should he do? Should he chance getting off the mule and leaving the supplies on the porch?

When the dog did nothing but stick its head out from under the porch, Jacob slid from the mule and unloaded his packs. He stacked everything except the dress by the door. These people needed them more than the Lillies. Jacob would pay them back some other way. He eyed the stack of wood next to the house and knew he'd be back at the first opportunity to chop more.

By the time he reached the Lillie yard, the snow began to fall in earnest. Fingers numb, he knocked on the door to let them know he'd be heading home.

Phoebe answered. "You don't have to knock anymore. You're considered family."

Maybe so, but until Phoebe declared her love for him, he would never actually be a member of the family. "I'm heading back to my cabin for the night. Wanted y'all to know so you wouldn't worry."

"Pa's been wondering where you were today?"

"I went and dropped some supplies off at the Coffman place." He waited for her condemnation. Instead, she nodded.

"That was kind of you. Eli's mother isn't capable of doing much."

Phoebe had started to thaw over the last couple of days, but her acceptance of his kind deed toward the family of the man she detested, gave Jacob hope that he'd have the woman he loved back very soon.

He wanted very much to kiss her. To pull her in his arms and stare into those eyes. Instead, he shoved his hands in his pockets and headed back to the mule.

"Jacob, wait." Phoebe dashed after him. "Won't you stay for supper?"

"No, my cabin will be freezing as it is. I've work to do in order to start school back on Monday and a fire to get going." He clenched his fists to keep from brushing his knuckles across her cheek.

"Wait here." She hurried back into the house. A few minutes later, she returned with a crock. "Hot soup and some cornbread. Don't say no. You'll need it to warm you while you get a fire started."

"Thank you." He climbed on the mule before reaching down for the food. "I'll be by tomorrow to see how JJ is doing."

"Jacob."

"Yes?"

"Thank you. For everything."

*

She didn't think her words were enough. How could four words convey everything she felt, everything she meant? She loved him with every fiber of her being. Could he still love her after the way she'd treated him?

Even a godly man such as Jacob had his limits, and Phoebe could very well have pushed him to the very edge of what he could endure. Her heart dropped as he rode away, disappearing in the falling snow.

She turned and went back inside to take her turn

with JJ. He was sitting up in bed for the first time since being shot. He plucked at the covers, but grinned when he saw her.

"How are you feeling?"

He shrugged, then winced. "All right, if I don't move. Will you play the mandolin for me?"

"I don't sing anymore." She twisted her hands in her skirt, realizing another thing Eli had taken from her. Forgiving the man would not be easy.

"Please? I'm so bored sitting here and Grandma is always fussing over me with this or that." His young face fell, wrenching at Phoebe's heart.

How could she deny him when he lay there because of an unwise choice she made? "I'll try." She retrieved the instrument from a shelf and sat in the rocker next to the bed.

With the mandolin on her lap, she plucked a sad, romantic tune handed down through the generations. She closed her eyes and pictured Jacob's face and pretended to sing only to him. Instead of increasing her pain, the melody was healing, the lyrics speaking of romance and faith that better things would come.

Tears poured down her face as she sang and the words trembled.

"Don't cry. It's beautiful." JJ patted her arm.

She opened her eyes. "I needed to sing again. Thank you for asking me to."

"It's been too long since I've seen you happy,"

he said. "You used to be the sunshine in this house. Poor baby Maggie is starting to act like you. Callie does her best to mother the baby, but it isn't the same."

"I'm sorry. I have been full of myself, haven't I?" She set the mandolin aside and hugged him. "I promise to do better."

"Just find what makes you happy and hold on to it." He slid down the pillows. "I'm going to sleep now. Wake me when supper's done."

Phoebe planted a kiss on his forehead, knowing her fifteen-year-old brother would never allow her to if he were well and able. "When did you get so wise?" She whispered.

The others were already sitting down to supper. Phoebe would give JJ his after he slept awhile.

"It was good to hear you sing, daughter." Pa clapped a hand on her shoulder. "Sounded like old times. You remind me so much of your ma."

"Thank you. That's a wonderful compliment." Phoebe took her place at the table.

"You ready to finish that quilt?" Grandma asked, setting a bowl of soup in front of her. "It's time to start working on a wedding quilt. Someday, you'll wed and –"

Phoebe drowned out her words. She wouldn't marry anyone unless it was Jacob. She eyed the Old Maid's Rambling hanging on the rack. That would be her quilt if she didn't find a way to tell him of her feelings.

The hot chicken soup burned the roof of her mouth and warmed her better than the fire in the stone fireplace. Grandma had left the shutters open and snow fell bringing with it bitter cold and beauty.

"Makes everything pure again, doesn't it?" Grandma said following Phoebe's gaze. "Just like God's mercy."

Phoebe was finally ready to accept the words her grandmother said. She hated the bitterness in her heart. Maybe she'd even go as far as to ask Jacob to let her accompany him when he went back to check on the Coffmans. The children weren't responsible for their father's deeds.

How was Viola faring? She thought often of her sister after their hugging session. Phoebe prayed she was adjusting to married life in a crowded cabin. "Pa?"

"Yep."

"When you marry the Widow Williams, and she moves in here, why don't you give Viola and her husband the widow's cabin? It can't be good all those people shoved into one place."

Pa stared at her as if she'd sprouted horns. "I reckon that sounds like a good idea, but who gave you the notion I plan on getting hitched?"

Phoebe cocked her head. "We aren't stupid."

"Well, there are still things to take care of

before I can consider getting married." He finished his soup and went to sit by the fire.

Pa was right. There was still the matter of Eli and the sheriff. That meant Phoebe shouldn't plan on revealing her feelings to Jacob just yet. None of them needed the distraction. She stood and helped Callie clear the table while Grandma sat with her feet up in front of the fire. Phoebe could see her swollen ankles from where she stood and vowed to do more around the house until Pa brought another woman home.

While she washed the dishes, she watched the snow fall and wondered how Jacob was faring in the cold? Had his cabin warmed up yet? What would it be like to care for just him? To someday see their children sitting around the table in a cozy cabin?

She shook her head. Silly dreaming. With nothing settled, that's all it was. Dreams. Plus, it was a daily battle to squelch her desire for revenge against Eli for all the trouble he's done. Not only the rape, but his association with a crooked sheriff who thought nothing of shooting a boy.

She lowered her head and prayed for the strength to continuously turn the matter over to God. Finished, she turned to look at her pa. "Did you contact anyone about the sheriff shooting JJ?"

"Yes, I did. Haven't got a response yet, but it takes a while all the way from Little Rock. Don't fret. It's taken care of." Pa toed off his boots and wiggled his toes in front of the fire. "But, I'm still hoping for a shot at the man myself, God forgive me."

He'd have to forgive them both, because Phoebe had the same revengeful thought.

20

Phoebe gathered the last of the few eggs and glanced at the two in her basket. With four eggs, they weren't enough for a meal. Maybe Grandma could make pancakes for breakfast instead, or everyone's favorite, chocolate gravy. They had a bit of flour and sugar left.

As she latched the gate to the chicken coop, Jacob burst from the trees. She dropped the basket and shrieked. "You scared me." The eggs lay in pieces, their ooze soaking into the ground.

Jacob grabbed her hand. "That's nothing. Get in the house. Where are the children?" He dragged her full speed toward the back door.

"What's happening?" She glanced over her shoulder to see a group of men, Eli and Sheriff Johnson included, emerge from the trees, rifles propped on their shoulders. Her heart stopped. So it had come to this. They planned to shoot the Lillies from their home.

Jacob thrust her inside and bolted the door.

"Ben, get the children into the loft, and move JJ from the back room. Trouble is coming."

Without another word, the children scampered up the ladder, and JJ emerged from the bedroom. "I'm here, and I can shoot."

"No." Phoebe put a hand to her mouth and shook her head. "You're still in pain."

"I owe them one." He shuffled to the mantel and pulled down Pa's shotgun. Tossing it to his father, he grabbed the other two leaning against the wall and handed one to Phoebe. "Jacob, you going to shoot that gun on your hip."

Jacob paled. "I don't have a choice, but it won't be much good against rifles."

"Here." Pa handed him his rifle and pulled his hog leg from a chest in the corner. "Us hill folk have guns a plenty."

The rifle was heavy in Phoebe's arms. She grabbed two boxes of shells and handed a handful to each of them. "What now?"

"We wait." Pa stuffed his shells into the pocket on the bib of his overalls. "We won't be the first to shoot."

"Maybe I can talk to them. Eli might still want to marry me. He might listen." They couldn't hole up in the cabin while bullets flew. What if one of the children was hit? What about Grandma?

Grandma had already pulled another rifle from under the sink. "I'm ready. Been a long time since

I've shot a varmint."

"No, ma. The recoil will knock you on your backside." Pa took the gun from her. "As much as I appreciate the thought, the children need you."

"Please, Grandma." Tears ran down Phoebe's cheeks.

"Okay, but just so y'all know, I ain't too old to pull that trigger." She dragged her feet, then labored up the ladder. "I could shoot from up here just fine."

And draw fire to the upper floor. They couldn't let that happen. Maggie's wails filled the cabin and a shot had yet to be fired.

"Ben Lillie!" Eli's shout reached through the closed door. "Y'all leave peaceful like and we can avoid any more bloodshed."

"This is my home, and you're trespassing." Pa leaned his shoulder against the door frame.

"You betrayed us, Ben."

"You're doing wrong. All of you."

Phoebe clutched her Pa's arm. "Tell them you've contacted the authorities in Little Rock. Shouldn't they be here by now?"

"It snowed a foot last night." Pa shook her loose. "We can't count on them."

Her blood ran cold. These thin walls wouldn't stop a bullet. "We need to pile the furniture in front of us."

"I'm already on it." Jacob flipped the kitchen table on its side. The sound as he pushed it across the floor grated on Phoebe's ears.

She glanced at the back door, thankful to see he'd piled what little could be moved. A few chests and a bed. She prayed it would be enough. "What if they try burning us out?"

"Then, God help us, we'll try shooting our way free."

The children. Nausea boiled in her stomach. She took deep breaths to calm herself and prayed for God's intervention.

"My young'uns are in here, Eli. Have you no shame?" Pa pointed to where he wanted Phoebe and Jacob to station themselves. The house had only two windows. Pa took one and they took the other.

Phoebe met Jacob's determined gaze. "Can you do this?"

"Can you?" He shrugged. "After accidentally killing a woman, I swore to never point my gun at another person again. Now, here I am."

"Technically, it's Pa's gun." She gave him a sad grin. What if they died today? She'd never told him she still loved him. "Jacob, I—" A bullet whizzed past her head.

JJ ducked and grabbed his side. "It hurts to move. I need to find a place to shoot from that I don't have to duck."

"Guard the back. Make sure no one is sneaking up us. Make every shot count," Pa said, aiming his rifle through the window. "Shoot and duck."

JJ nodded and duck-walked to the back of the cabin, his face etched in pain.

Phoebe's ears rang with the volley of shots. So far, it looked as if both sides were doing nothing but showing their hand. Either that or every one of them was a bad shot. She aimed more carefully, lining up her sight, and shot one of the men she didn't know in the foot. He dropped his gun and hollered, rolling on the ground.

"Good one." Pa grinned. "Took him down without killing him. I doubt we'll get that lucky with Eli or the sheriff. Mr. Wright, you need to take better aim and stop wasting my ammunition. I know how you feel about shooting, but these men will shoot you as soon look at you."

"I reckon I can do that. Hit them in the leg, I mean."

Phoebe turned to tell Jacob to stifle down his fear when a bullet whizzed through the window and tore through her skirt. She screamed and fell to the floor, fire burning through her leg. "Pa, I'm hit."

She didn't want to die this way, shot by the same fiend who had raped her. She closed her eyes and prayed as the circle of blood under her spread.

"Dear, Lord, help my girl," Pa prayed, too. "Jacob, can you do anything?

If anyone on earth could help her, it would be Jacob. She trusted him with everything in her.

*

"I'll tend to her. Keep shooting." Jacob dragged Phoebe away from the window and ripped a larger hole in her skirt.

"Stop it." Her eyes snapped open, and she slapped his hands and tried to hold the torn pieces of bloody fabric together. "It's not right for you to see my bare leg, and this is, was, my favorite dress."

"Don't be foolish. I measured for your shoe, remember? And I bought you a new dress."

"That was the lower part and was covered by my stockings." She hissed as he wiped at the blood.

"It's just a graze, but the bleeding needs to be stopped, and you probably need stitches when we're out of here." He thought his heart had stopped when she'd screamed and fell. At that moment, he'd forgotten about his resolve not to shoot another person. Blood lust filled him to see her in pain.

"Tie something around it, so I can get back to my window." Phoebe scowled.

"You should sit out of the way."

"I'm needed. So are you."

Jacob tied a dishtowel around her leg and helped her to her feet. "Stay out of sight at least."

"I have to poke my head up once in a while or I can't see. They got me when I got distracted. That won't happen again." She shook her head as if he were an imbecile. A second later, her look softened. "Did you say you bought me a dress? Jacob, if I don't make it out of—"

He gripped her shoulders, leaving bloody handprints on the flowered fabric. "Don't say it." If she said the words 'out alive', then they might come true. "We'll talk when this over."

"If Phoebe is all right, I could use some help here," Ben said. "I'm outnumbered."

"Want me to come over there, Pa?" JJ asked. "There's nothing happening back here."

"No." The three adults shouted at the same time.

Jacob peered out the window, Phoebe on the other side. She stood with her injured leg bent and bit her bottom lip. The Lillies were made of steel. Ben had taken down another one, this man holding his shoulder. "There're two men missing."

"Yep." Ben nodded. "That's who my boy needs to be looking for. Eli is a snake and will do anything to achieve his goal."

The children screamed overhead. Jacob rushed for the ladder just as a man fell out of the loft.

Grandma leaned down. "He climbed up the oak tree, so I pushed him out of the loft. Nobody scares my babies. Doesn't look like he's getting up anytime soon. Doubt he's dead, though." She withdrew out of sight.

Jacob's eyes widened. "Uh, JJ, tie him up."

These people were the stuff legends were made of. The type of people who settled this great country. He couldn't hold a candle to even an old woman born and raised in the mountains. Resolved to do his share, he resumed his place at the window, and aimed. His shot took a man in the thigh. *Lord, forgive me.*

"This is taking too long." They needed to do something. *Think, man. You were a police officer. This isn't your first standoff.* The tree. If a man could come up, then one could go down. "I'm going out the loft window. JJ, cover me."

"No, Jacob." Phoebe's faced paled. "They'll kill you."

"I have to stop this before someone is killed." He picked up his pistol from the table and shoved it into his waistband. He marched to her side, took her face in his hands, and kissed her. Not the sweetness of a first kiss, but the hard demanding one of a man who might not see the woman he loved again. "I love you." He put his forehead against hers.

"Oh, Jacob, I love you, too. I always have. Come back to me."

"I will." He didn't promise. Only God knew whether his plan would work.

He climbed the ladder, meeting Phoebe's glance one last time before facing Grandma and the children. They watched silently, even baby Maggie kept quiet, as he reached out the window and grabbed the nearest tree trunk. He tuned and studied each of their dear faces, thankful, that for a few months at least, he'd had a family. God willing, he still would have one at the end of the day.

He sat on the windowsill, and then kicked away from the house. He dangled twenty feet above the ground before swinging his legs up and wrapping them around the trunk. Please, God, don't let anyone come around the corner of the house. He'd be a sitting turkey.

21

Jacob raced for the cover of the trees, what little there was with winter set in. His boots left prints in the snow. Nothing he could do about it except pray no one saw.

He made a wide berth, keeping his eyes peeled for a way to sneak up behind Eli and the sheriff without getting shot by one of the Lillies. He didn't want to think about what would happen if one of their shots missed its original target.

A twig snapped under his boot, and he froze. Would they think it only a limb breaking under the weight of the snow? He held his breath. When no shot of alarm came, he continued his slow journey around the clearing.

"You can't win this fight, Eli." Ben's shout rang across the yard. "You're down to two."

"We can stay out here all week if we have to. Eventually, you'll run out of food or firewood."

"It's pretty cold out here," Sheriff Johnson hissed. "I don't relish continuing this standoff for much longer. What if the feds come? We need to skip the state. Set up a still somewhere else."

Jacob peered around a pine tree. As long as the two were arguing, they weren't shooting. He pulled his pistol.

"What the …" Eli took a step back.

Coming from around the Lillie place was the Widow Williams, Viola and her husband, and several of the other hill families, all armed. They took up residence in front of the house and faced in Eli's direction.

Ben whipped open the front door and stepped outside. "What now, Eli? You going to shoot everyone here?"

Eli and the sheriff whirled to run, only to stare down the barrel of Jacob's pistol.

"Game's over, boys. Drop your weapons."

They cursed and dropped the rifles.

"Now, mosey on out there and say howdy to your neighbors." Jacob motioned with the pistol. "We'll all be real friendly."

*

Phoebe limped onto the front porch, tears running down her face at the sight of Jacob herding Eli and the sheriff. The other men might have gotten away, but they'd be found, and the hollow would be a safe place to live again.

"You're hurt?" Viola helped her to a chair on the porch. "I'll send John for the doctor."

"In a minute. I want to see the end of all this."

"What do you want me to do with them?" Jacob poked his pistol in Eli's back, causing the man to stumble.

"I'd like to shoot them," Ben said. "But I've chosen mercy instead. They can't help the fact they're fools. Phoebe, you want to say anything?"

She struggled to her feet and forced herself forward. Holding onto Viola, she made her way down the stairs, and then refused any more help. The few feet it took to stand in front of Eli seemed like a mile, and her body trembled from the effort.

"I've nothing to say, Pa. But this." She reared back her fist and landed a solid punch to Eli's jaw. Shaking the pain from her hand, she met Jacob's amused gaze, and winked. "I feel better now."

Viola rushed forward to help her back to her seat. "You bloodied his lip."

"Good." Phoebe laughed, feeling more freedom than she had in weeks. "Oh, that felt good."

"Did you break your hand?"

"I don't think so. Get me a bucket of snow, and I'll be fine."

The sound of an engine reached her ears and turned her head to see a car barreling in their direction. Two officers in federal uniform climbed out as soon as the vehicle stopped.

"These the men you wired about?" One asked, glancing around the group. "Looks like a war zone."

"It was," Pa said. "A couple crawled away, wounded, but they won't die. We'll give you their names, and you can round them up. We sure are glad to see you boys." He shook each of their hands.

JJ came outside and leaned against Phoebe's chair. "Nobody died. That's good. The man inside is awake now."

"Officers, there's a man tied up in the house. He's yours," she said, leaning her head back. "I think I could use the doctor now."

Viola raced to her husband's side and within seconds he had dashed down the road. "He's a good man, Phoebe. I hope y'all come to accept him."

"As long as he treats you right, we'll be fine." She laid her head back and closed her eyes.

"Sweetheart?" She opened her eyes to see Jacob kneeling in front of her. "Let me get you into the house." He scooped her into his arms. The safest place in the world for her.

She laid her cheek against his broad chest and listened to his heartbeat. Thankful for each thump. He'd made it back alive and risked his life for her and her family. She was a blessed woman indeed.

Jacob carried her into the bedroom and laid her on the bed that had seen so much pain and recovery lately. "At least they shot my bad leg." She gave a shaky laugh.

He shook his head, his eyes shimmering. "I thought I'd lost you for a moment. Once the doctor arrives, you'll be as good as new."

"Tell that to the pain."

He knelt beside the bed and gripped her hands. "Marry me, Phoebe. Marry me the minute you're back on your feet."

"I'll stand up now if you want. Where's that dress you bought me?"

"Why?" He frowned.

She smiled. "Because I want it to be my wedding dress."

His tears escaped, and she pulled one hand free of his to wipe them away. "I thank God for sending you to us, Jacob Wright."

"Even though I wounded your pride almost immediately?" He grinned and wiped his face on his shoulder.

"Even though." She cupped his cheek. "We've been through a lot, haven't we? God has brought me out of despair and into the light. I was so hungry for revenge, thinking it would be sweet, but instead it filled my heart and mind with bitterness. I was blind to everything else, even your love. Will you forgive me?"

"There's nothing to forgive." He held her hand to his cheek. "I'm glad you didn't stop loving me. I would never have stopped trying to win back your love. You're my golden-haired girl of the Ozarks. My sunshine."

"You're such a poet." She laughed, and glanced

up as the doctor rushed into the room.

"I seem to be coming out here quite often, Miss Lillie." He set his bag on the foot of the bed.

"Hopefully, no longer." Jacob stood. "I'll wait right outside the door. Call me if you need anything."

"I will." She laid back and closed her eyes, gritting her teeth against the pain as the doctor ministered to her leg.

22

J acob sent this." Viola handed Phoebe a brown paper wrapped parcel.

"It's my dress." She hadn't seen it yet, and he'd been insistent that she not receive the gift until their wedding day. Silly man. What if it didn't fit?

She tore at the paper and pulled out the prettiest dress she'd ever seen. The color matched her eyes. A sheer lace overdress of blue covered a satin underdress in the same shade. "It's beautiful." While the lace part of the dress was a rounded neckline, the under part was cut into a V. Gathered lace formed a belt around the waist.

"You'll look as pretty as a spring day." Viola helped her into the dress, which fit perfectly.

A knock on the door announced Pa's arrival. He carried a black velvet pouch. "These were your ma's. No better day to give them to you." His red-rimmed eyes were a testimony to his emotion.

Phoebe opened the bag. Inside were her mother's pearls. A necklace and earrings. "Really? These are mine?"

He nodded. "She always said they'd go to you on your wedding day." He gathered her into his arms. "You're marrying a right fine man."

"You and the widow Williams will be married soon. You won't even miss me."

"That's a falsehood." He rested his chin on the top of her head. "You've been the rock of this household since your ma died."

"I'll be right down the road." Jacob planned on expanding the teacher's cabin, but the small place would work fine until he had time. A cozy little place for newlyweds. Her face heated at the thought.

She wasn't ignorant of what went on between married couples, and her ordeal with Eli filled in a lot of missing pieces of what when on between a man and a woman, unfortunately. "I'm scared, Pa."

He held her at arm's length. "Of what? Are you changing your mind?"

"No." She bit her bottom lip. "After Eli, what if I can't—"

"Shh. Jacob is a loving man. He will be gentle and so filled with reverence of you being his wife, you won't think or feel anything but him."

She searched his eyes. "Truly?"

"I promise." He kissed her forehead. "A man like that can erase a lot of grief."

She hoped so. Although she'd come a long way since that horrible night, she still didn't feel worthy of such a fine man. One that refused to look the other way when she was at her most unlovable.

"Oh." Grandma stepped into the room and put a hand to her mouth. "You look as lovely as your ma did on her wedding day." She held out a filmy veil. "This was also your ma's." She pinned it into Phoebe's hair.

Phoebe glanced in the mirror. The veil softened her features and flowed around her shoulders. Pearls seemed to float around the edges. "Thank you."

Pa pulled Grandma and Viola into their circle. "It's time. Jacob won't wait forever." He winked at Phoebe.

"Yes, he will." She smiled. Her man had proven he'd wait as long as it takes.

Pa crooked his arm and led her to the front door. Phoebe peeked out the window. The yard was unrecognizable with the early greenery of spring. Somehow, white fabric had been draped around everything that didn't move. At the end of the yard, through several rows of benches, stood a white lattice arch. Under the arch waited the handsomest man, and he waited for her.

She blinked back tears and smiled up at Pa. "I'm ready now."

*

Jacob caught his breath as Phoebe stepped out the door. He'd made the right choice with the dress. She was exquisite.

Someone played a soft tune on a flute as she made her way to him, his vision blurred by tears. He blinked them away, not wanting to miss a single moment of her approach. They'd wanted to get married immediately after the arrest of Eli and the sheriff, but Ben had insisted they have a proper courting time to make sure they really loved each other after the horrors of the past months.

Ben clapped him on the shoulder as he slipped his daughter's hand into Jacob's. "Take care of my child."

Jacob nodded and took a deep shuddering breath. They were moments away from him receiving the best gift God could ever give him. He wanted time to speed up as much as he wanted it to slow.

The pastor stepped in front of them as the guests settled into place. The sun perched on the treetops, ready to make its descent, streaking the indigo sky with pumpkin and coral.

"Dearly beloved, we are gathered here today..."

Jacob tried to concentrate on the pastor's words, but he found it hard to notice anything but the beauty in front of him. A woman so strong, so full of love for her family, he wondered what she saw in him, and thanked God every day that she saw something worthwhile enough to bind herself to him.

"Jacob Wright, do you take this woman—"

"I do."

"I wasn't finished, but all right." The pastor laughed along with the guests. "I've met eager grooms before."

"Just hurry up. I'd like to kiss my bride."

"Do you Phoebe Faith Lillie, take this man to be your lawful wedded husband. To have and to hold from this day forward, in sickness and in health..."

"I do." Her hands trembled in his.

They exchanged rings, the simple gold band Jacob had bought slipping perfectly over her small finger. She beamed at him through her veil and mouthed that she loved him.

His heart swelled. Jacob had no doubt they'd be together until death parted them. They'd already weathered so much. Her middle name suited her. Funny that he'd never thought to ask her middle name. Maybe there was a story there. One he could ask her about later.

"I now pronounce you husband and wife. Mr. Wright, you may kiss your bride."

Jacob lifted her veil and cupped her face, gazing into her eyes for a moment before he wrapped his arms around her and pulled her to him. He lowered his head, placing his lips over hers and taking a taste of heaven.

A white dove flew overhead, and his heart soared.

The End

ABOUT THE AUTHOR

www.cynthiahickey.com

Cynthia Hickey is a multi-published and best-selling author of cozy mysteries and romantic suspense. She has taught writing at many conferences and small writing retreats. She and her husband run the publishing press, Winged Publications. They live in Arizona and Arkansas, becoming snowbirds with three dogs. They have ten grandchildren who keep them busy and tell everyone they know that "Nana is a writer."